IN
WARTIME

The Award-Winning Classic

'Most of us have enjoyed lives of peace and freedom and plenty. Here is a fine book, supremely well written, that takes us back to a time, not that long ago, when Holland lived through a terrible winter of hunger and occupation and war. It's a book we should all read, to remind us never to take our freedom and peace and plenty for granted'

Michael Morpurgo, author of *War Horse*

'A vivid, captivating portrait of life and resistance during the German occupation in the Netherlands. The strength and courage of the characters is sure to inspire a new generation of readers'

R.M. Romero   *akow*

'It's an amazing story ⸱   're at
all interested in WWI

D1351143

Books

'This is a fantastic novel that tells a side of WWII that hasn't been told much before in children's literature... There is danger, heartache and mystery'

Books Your Kids Will Love

JAN TERLOUW was born in the Netherlands in 1931. He worked as a nuclear physicist in countries across the world before entering politics as a representative of the Dutch D66 party in 1971. Alongside his political career he has written many successful children's books, including *Winter in Wartime*, which was based on his own memories of the Nazi occupation. It won the Golden Pen Prize for the best Dutch children's book in 1973 and has since been adapted for film and stage.

LAURA WATKINSON is a full-time translator from Dutch, Italian and German, and has also translated Tonke Dragt's *The Letter for the King, The Secrets of the Wild Wood, The Song of Seven* and *The Goldsmith and the Master Thief* for Pushkin Children's Books. She lives in Amsterdam.

WINTER
IN
WARTIME

JAN TERLOUW

Translated by Laura Watkinson

Pushkin Children's

Pushkin Press
71–75 Shelton Street
London, WC2H 9JQ

Winter in Wartime was first published as
Oorlogswinter in The Netherlands, 1973

First published by Pushkin Press in 2018

This edition first published in 2019

This publication has been made possible with financial
support from the Dutch Foundation for Literature.

N ederlands
letterenfonds
dutch foundation
for literature

1 3 5 7 9 8 6 4 2

ISBN 13: 978-1-78269-183-9

Designed and typeset by Tetragon, London
Printed and bound by CPI Group (UK) Ltd, Croydon CRO 4YY

www.pushkinpress.com

I

It was such a dark, dark night.

Step by step, holding out one hand in front of him, Michiel made his way along the cycle path at the side of the track. In his other hand, he was carrying a cotton bag with two bottles of milk inside.

New moon, and really cloudy too, he thought. *But I must be somewhere near Van Ommen's farm by now.* He peered to the right but, no matter how hard he tried, he couldn't see anything. *Next time I'm not going unless I can take the dynamo torch. Erica can just make sure she's home by half-past seven. This isn't going to end well.*

He was soon proved right. Even though he was walking so very slowly and carefully, the bag still smashed into one of the posts that were meant to stop the farmers' carts driving onto the cycle path. Blast it! Carefully, he felt the bag. Wet! One of the bottles was broken. What a waste of precious milk. In a foul mood, and even more cautiously than before, he started walking again. Goodness, it was so dark that he could hardly see anything at all. He was only about five hundred yards from home and knew the way like the back of his hand. Even so, being inside before eight was going to be a challenge.

Wait a minute, though—he could see the vaguest shimmer of light over there. Yes, that was right, the Bogaards' place. They weren't too careful about the blackout. But they didn't have much more to hide than the light of a candle anyway. He knew there were no other posts until the road now, though, and once he was there it would be easier. There were more houses, and a little light usually managed to escape somehow or other. Oh yuck, there was milk dripping into his clog. Was that footsteps he could hear? Not likely, it was on the stroke of eight. And everyone had to be inside their houses by then. He could feel a different surface beneath his feet. The main road. Now he had to turn right and just be careful not to end up in the ditch. Yes, it was easier now, as he'd expected. Very, very dimly, he could see the outline of the houses. The De Ruiters' house, Miss Doeven's, the Zomers', the blacksmith's, the Green Cross building. He was almost home.

Then, just in front of him, an electric torch flashed on, shining right into his eyes. He nearly jumped out of his skin.

"*Es ist* after eight o'clock," said a voice. "Now you are my prisoner. *Was ist das* in your hand? A grenade?"

"Turn that bloody torch off, Dirk," said Michiel. "Why'd you want to go and startle me like that?"

He'd recognized the voice, even with the fake German accent. It was their neighbours' son. Dirk Knopper was fond of silly jokes—or at least his idea of a joke.

8

He was twenty-one years old and he wasn't scared of anything.

"A bit of a fright, eh? It'll toughen you up," he said. "Anyway, it's true. It's gone eight. If a German comes along, he'll shoot you dead as a threat to the German Reich. *Heil Hitler*!"

"Ssh! Don't go yelling that name around."

"What's the problem?" Dirk said casually. "Our occupiers like hearing Hitler's name, don't they?"

They walked on together. Dirk shielded the torch with his hand, so that only a little light slipped through, but it still seemed like broad daylight to Michiel. He could see the roadside clearly now, which felt like a luxury.

"Hey, how did you get hold of that torch? Not to mention the batteries."

"Stole it from the Krauts."

"Yeah, a likely story," scoffed Michiel.

"No, really. You know we've got two officers billeted with us, right? Well, the other day, one of them—the fat one, you know—had a cardboard box in his room with what must have been about ten of these torches in there. Well, I say *his* room, but I mean *our* room, of course. And so I... liberated one."

"You just went wandering into his room?"

"Yeah, of course. I always pop in when they're not around, just to check it out. No trouble at all. The only person I have to watch out for is my dad. He's such a coward. If he knew I had this torch, he wouldn't be able to sleep a wink tonight. But he can't sleep anyway, because of Rinus de Raat. Right, there's my place. Bye, Michiel. Can you find your own way from here?"

"Yes, I'll manage. Bye!"

His clogs crunching on the gravel, Michiel walked through the front garden. He was glad Dirk hadn't noticed the broken bottle. He'd never have heard the last of it.

Inside the house, the carbide lamp was still burning away brightly. It was always like that early in the evening, when Father had just recently filled it. That was a nasty job, because of the smell. But once the metal pot was closed and the flame was burning, the smell went away and the lamp gave off about as much light as an electric one. Unfortunately, though, as the evening went on, the light grew weaker and by half-past nine only a tiny blue flame remained, just enough to stop you from tripping over the furniture.

Michiel would have liked to read in the evenings. There was plenty of light all day long, but he had no time then. At night, when he did have time—no light. He'd discovered eighteen yellowing books by Jules Verne in his father's bookcase, and he was longing to read them. At the beginning of the evening, you could read if you were within a couple of yards of the lamp, but later on you could only make out the words by holding the book right up to the little blue flame. It wouldn't have been fair to hog the light though, particularly not when there were guests—and there were nearly always guests.

The front room was packed tonight too. In addition to Mother, Father, Erica and Jochem, Michiel saw at least ten other people. Glancing around, he didn't recognize any of them, except for Uncle Ben. Mother introduced him to everyone. There was a married couple, Mr and Mrs Van der Heiden, who told Michiel he'd sat on their laps when he was little. They came from Vlaardingen, so it was possible, as that was where he'd been born. Then there was a very old lady with wrinkles, who said she was his Aunt Gerdien and demanded a kiss from him. He didn't even know he had an Aunt Gerdien. Mother explained that she was a very distant cousin of Father's, and that Father had last seen the good woman twenty years ago. Only she didn't quite put it that way. Then there were two unfamiliar ladies who remarked on how very tall he'd grown, plus a smug little man who had the nerve to call him "lad" even though Michiel was almost sixteen, and a few others. Except for the "lad" fellow, they all seemed to know exactly who he was.

"They've done their homework," muttered Michiel.

All the visitors came from the west of the country, the famine having driven them to the east and the north. It was early winter 1944–45, and there was a war on. That meant there was barely anything left to eat in the big cities. There was no transport either, so everyone had to walk. Sometimes dozens, sometimes hundreds of miles.

They made their way along the roads with handcarts, prams, bikes without proper tyres, and all kinds of other strange contraptions. There was a curfew too, so by eight o'clock the streets had to be empty. That made it essential to have friends and acquaintances who lived somewhere along the route. Michiel's parents had previously had no idea they knew so many people—or rather, that so many people knew them.

Night after night, at around seven o'clock, the bell would ring and keep ringing for the next hour. Some stranger would be standing there on the doorstep, beaming at them and exclaiming, "Hello! How are you? You remember me, don't you? Miep, from The Hague. I've thought about you so often." It would have been amusing if it weren't so very sad. Miep would turn out to be a lady who'd been introduced to Father and Mother as Mrs Van Druten on one occasion at the home of a mutual acquaintance. However, when you saw that Miep was malnourished and exhausted, and heard that she'd walked all the way from The Hague in a pair of worn-out gym shoes, just to fetch a few potatoes from Overijssel for her daughter's children, then you said, "Of course, Aunt Miep! Come on in. How are you?" and you gave her a bowl of pea soup and a chair by the lamp, and a bed for the night, or at least a mattress on the floor.

When Michiel had said hello to everyone, he asked his mother to come into the kitchen with him, lighting the way with the torch. It worked like a bicycle dynamo, and was powered by manually pumping the handle, which produced a fairly decent beam of light, but also tired out your thumb. "I'm sorry, Mother. I broke a bottle."

"Oh, Michiel. Couldn't you have been a bit more careful?"

Michiel stopped using the torch and lifted the blackout blind. The darkness was as black as ink.

"Well, there's no moon tonight, see, and I didn't have the torch," he said apologetically. He lowered the blind and began pumping the torch again, so that they had a little light.

His mother was already regretting her remark. She stroked Michiel's hair.

He's doing a man's work, she thought. *Going out in the pitch darkness all on his own to fetch milk, which I'd be too scared to do. And all I'm doing is shouting at him.*

"I'm sorry, Michiel," she said. "It just slipped out. I know it wasn't your fault. I'm just thinking about all those people in there who are waiting for their coffee."

Coffee? That was stretching it. What they drank was ersatz coffee, a substitute with brown colouring, and the hot milk was needed to make it drinkable.

"I can't go back again," said Michiel. "It's past eight. If you could hold the torch and give me some light, I'll take the broken glass out of the bag."

"Leave it until tomorrow. Would you hand me the other bottle? Thanks. So how did it happen?"

13

"Hit a post, near Van Ommen's place. Shall I pour the milk into the saucepan?"

"Here, I'll do it."

Michiel took back the dynamo torch and they returned to the front room to heat the milk on the stove. There'd been no coal for a long time now, so they had to use blocks of wood in the stove instead.

When they'd finished their coffee, the guests began to tell stories about life in the big cities. Hunger, cold and fear—those were the main topics of conversation. The shortages. The uncertainty. Everyone had a story about a family member who'd had to go into hiding, or a friend who'd been dragged off to a concentration camp, or a house that had been destroyed by a bomb. Then they moved on to the rumours about the war—about Patton, the American general who was making such good progress on the Western Front, and about the losses the Germans were suffering on the Eastern Front, or so people said.

Then there were jokes about the war. Rumour had it that Anton Mussert, the leader of the Dutch pro-Nazi NSB organization, was married to his aunt. Mr Van der Heiden told them a story about a newsreel clip of Mussert being shown at the cinema. Someone at the front had called out: "Anton!", and a high-pitched voice at the back had replied: "Yes, Auntie?"

That cheered them all up a bit, and Uncle Ben said, "Have you heard the one about Goering, Goebbels and Hitler having a bet to see who could stay in a room with a polecat the longest? Goering tries it first. Fifteen minutes later, he leaves the room, gagging. Then Goebbels. He manages half an hour. Finally, Hitler goes in. Five minutes later, the polecat comes running out!"

They were so tense and miserable that such simple jokes were all it took to fill the room with laughter.

The carbide lamp was almost dead by now. Clutching stumps of candles, everyone shuffled off to bed or to a mattress on the floor. Michiel checked there was enough kindling wood for the stove tomorrow morning. He couldn't find another candle, and his mother had the torch, so he felt his way to his bedroom in the attic, got undressed and slipped into bed. Far in the distance, he heard the drone of an aeroplane.

"Rinus de Raat," mumbled Michiel. "I hope he doesn't fly our way."

Then he fell asleep, and slept right through that one thousand, six hundred and eleventh night of the German occupation.

2

When the German army, on the orders of their great *Führer*, Adolf Hitler, invaded the Netherlands and Belgium on 10th May 1940, Michiel van Beusekom was eleven. He remembered the radio broadcasting the thrilling news about parachute troops dropping over Ypenburg, repeat Ypenburg, and over Waalhaven, repeat Waalhaven. All day long, Dutch soldiers on horses passed through the village, joking with the girls and looking anything but heroic. Michiel, though, had secretly decided that war was a very exciting business, and he hoped it would go on for a long time.

He changed his mind soon enough. In fact, his first doubts came after only five days. That was when the Dutch army gave up the one-sided battle. Father turned pale when he heard the announcement on the radio, and Mother wept. Then there was all the worry about the boys from the village who'd joined the army. Fourteen of them in total. News soon came that eight of the lads were unharmed. They heard the same about three others a few days later. But there was still no news of the last three: Gerrit, the baker's son; Hendrik Bosser, who came from a farming family; and the Van Beusekoms' gardener's boy, who was known as Whitie, because his hair was so blond. Michiel could still remember it as if it were yesterday, sitting on the wheelbarrow for hours, watching Whitie's dad working in the garden. He said nothing—just kept working steadily. A week later, he went on working steadily, after Gerrit and Hendrik had turned up and there was still no sign of Whitie.

Gerrit had been captured. His fat face gleamed with glee as he told them about a German officer pointing in amazement at the freckles that covered his face from top to bottom.

"It's the rusty ends of my nerves of steel," he'd replied, a retort that made it feel as if they hadn't lost the war entirely after all.

It simply hadn't occurred to Hendrik Bosser to send a message home. But Whitie was buried at the Grebbeberg. His father went on weeding Mayor Van Beusekom's garden and didn't say a word.

Even then, so soon after that 10th of May, 1940, the young Michiel had realized his wish for the war to go on had been a foolish one. He wanted it to be over, the sooner the better—but that, too, was wishful thinking. The war had lasted for four years and five months now, and it was only getting worse. The Americans and the British had landed in France last June and were working to push back the Germans—they'd already advanced to the southern part of the Netherlands—but they hadn't made it across the rivers. They'd tried, at Arnhem. Sadly, though, the

Battle of Arnhem was won by the Germans. And now winter was on the way. A winter as black as pitch. The German occupiers, well aware that they were losing, were wreaking havoc. They seized almost everything that was edible and transported it to Germany. Famine broke out in the big cities. The Germans had lost control of the air. American and British planes flew around, shooting at every means of transportation they saw, and forcing the Germans to move at night, in the dark, which was no easy task.

The village of De Vlank, where Michiel's father was mayor, was on the northern edge of the Veluwe, near the town of Zwolle. The River IJssel ran between De Vlank and Zwolle, and it was an important strategic point, as there were two bridges across the IJssel, one for cars and one for the train. So the Allies were doing their utmost to smash the bridges. There was constant bombing. Destroying a bridge would cut off German transport routes.

The bridges had another important function besides allowing traffic to cross. They were a good place for stopping people and checking their papers. Young men could be arrested and sent to Germany to work in weapons factories. Individuals without valid identity papers could be caught. Yes, the Germans thought the IJssel Bridge was a very fine trap indeed.

As a result, travellers often stopped in De Vlank to ask if they would be able to cross the bridge safely, and how strict the checks were. It was well known that the mayor was no friend of the Germans, and that meant there was plenty of coming and going at the Van Beusekoms' house.

The morning after the night of the broken bottle, Michiel got up at half-past seven. There wasn't much point getting up earlier, because it was dark. So he thought he'd be the first one up and about, but no. Uncle Ben was already lighting the stove.

Uncle Ben wasn't his real uncle. Erica, Michiel and Jochem called him that as he was such a close family friend and he often came to visit them, usually staying for a few days. That would have been a problem with almost anyone else, because of the food. But not with Uncle Ben. He always managed to rustle something up. The last time he'd even got hold of half an ounce of pre-war tea for Mother and a cigar for Father.

"Morning, Uncle Ben."

"Oh, hello there, Michiel. I could do with a little help, chum. I need to get hold of a sack or two of potatoes today. Any idea where I can find some?"

"We could try Van de Bos. He lives right out in the sticks, a good half an hour's bike ride away. He's quite a long way from the main road, so he doesn't get many people coming by. I'll go with you."

"Thanks."

The room was getting nice and warm, with the stove roaring away. Michiel watched it suspiciously. The damp wood they usually had to make do with didn't burn that well. He lifted the lid of the old oak chest. Yes, it was empty. Uncle Ben had gone and put all the sticks of last resort in the stove.

"Hey, you've used up all the sticks of last resort," snapped Michiel.

"The *what*?"

"The sticks of last resort."

"And what exactly might they be?"

"Those thin, dry bits of kindling wood from the chest. Sometimes Mother gets a bit desperate. You know, when the stove looks like it's about to go out just before the food's cooked. Then she's allowed to use the wood from the chest. Father and I take it in turns to chop the wood very thin, and we put the sticks behind the stove to dry them out."

Uncle Ben gave him a guilty look. "I shall personally ensure the chest is filled again," he promised.

Michiel nodded. *That'll take you the best part of an hour*, he thought, but he didn't say anything. He didn't offer to do it for his uncle either. If he'd squandered the sticks of last resort, he'd have to suffer the consequences himself.

One by one, the guests rose from their beds. They were given two chewy slices of bread and a bowl of buttermilk porridge. Thanking Mrs Van Beusekom, they went on their way, some heading north, where they hoped to buy a sack of rye or potatoes, and others west, towards home, where their families were waiting for them, their bellies swollen with hunger.

When the family had finished their breakfast too, Uncle Ben asked Michiel if he'd go with him to Van de Bos's place now. Michiel gave the oak chest a meaningful look and said he had to take a couple of rabbits to Wessels first. Uncle Ben sighed, but then fetched an axe and headed out to the chopping block behind the shed. Michiel fed his thirty rabbits, then chose three of them, weighed them and left to go and see Wessels, determined to get at least fifteen guilders for them.

Michiel hadn't been to school for months now. Officially, he'd qualified for the fourth year of secondary school in Zwolle, but he couldn't get there now. The first day after the summer holiday, he'd attempted to go on the train. It had been an interesting journey. At Vlankenerbroek, an aeroplane had circled over the train. The driver had stopped and the passengers had got off and run into the fields, with the British plane speeding low above their heads. The British and American pilots weren't out to shoot Dutch citizens, though. They just wanted to disable all the German means of transportation.

When the passengers were far enough away, the plane dived low over the engine a few times, riddling it with bullets.

That was the end of the trips to Zwolle. The bike wasn't an option either, as there were no pneumatic tyres to be found. And going such a long way every day on wooden wheels simply wasn't practical. Besides, Michiel's parents thought it was too dangerous.

So, no school for Michiel, they decided. It was one of the very few things they'd decided for their son recently. The war had made Michiel more or less independent. He went out and returned with butter, eggs and bacon. He did jobs for the local farmers. He ran his own little business. He repaired broken wheelbarrows, handcarts and backpacks for the people who passed through from the cities. He knew where some Jewish people were hiding. He was fairly certain who had an illegal wireless. He knew Dirk was a member of the secret underground forces. But Michiel kept all this dangerous information to himself. He'd always been good at keeping quiet and he felt no need to go blabbing about what he knew.

When he returned from Wessels, seventeen guilders better off, he found his neighbour Dirk waiting by the garden gate.

"Morning."

"I need to speak to you," said Dirk. "In private."

"Let's go to the shed. What's the problem?"

But Dirk remained silent until they were inside.

"You sure no one can hear us?" he asked.

"Absolutely. There's no one around. It's safe here," said Michiel. "Anyway, everyone in our house can be trusted. So what's up?"

Dirk was looking a lot more serious than usual.

"Swear you won't tell anyone."

"I swear," said Michiel.

"Tonight," said Dirk, "three of us are going to make a raid on the rations office in Lagezande."

Lagezande was a village about four miles away from De Vlank.

Hearing about these secret plans gave Michiel a strange feeling in his stomach, but he acted as if it were all perfectly normal.

"You're raiding the rations office? What for?"

"Well, you know," Dirk explained, "there are lots of people in hiding around here. And they obviously don't get ration cards for bread, sugar, clothes, tobacco and that kind of thing."

Of course, it was almost impossible to buy anything without a ration card.

"I see," said Michiel.

"Good," said Dirk. "So we're going to raid the rations office, take all the cards, and share them out among the people who are hiding someone in their homes."

"How are you going to get into the safe?"

"I'm hoping Mr Van Willigenburg will be kind enough to open it for me."

"Who's Mr Van Willigenburg?"

"The director. He's a good chap. I know he's working late tonight. We'll go there and force him to open the safe and hand over the new ration cards. I'm counting on him not to resist too much."

"Who's we?"

"None of your business."

23

Michiel grinned. Dirk was right not to name any names.

"Why are you telling me all this?"

"Because I've got a letter here. If anything goes wrong, you need to give it to Bertus van Gelder. Will you do that?"

"Bertus? Is he in the resistance too?"

"You ask too many questions. Just give the letter to Bertus. That's all. OK?"

"Of course I will. But you don't think anything's going to go wrong, do you?"

"Probably not, but you never know. Do you have somewhere you can hide the letter?"

"Yes. Give it here."

Dirk took out an envelope from under his jumper. It was sealed and there was no name or address on it.

"So where are you going to hide it?"

"None of your business."

It was Dirk's turn to grin.

"I'll come back for it tomorrow," he said.

"OK. Don't get caught, Dirk."

"I won't. Take good care of the letter. Bye, then."

"Bye."

Whistling, Dirk left the shed. Michiel opened the door to the chicken coop. He took the straw out of the fourth nesting box from the right. The wooden board at the bottom was loose, so he lifted it and slid the letter underneath. Then he made everything look just as it was before. *No one's ever going to find that*, he thought to himself. Then he went up to his bedroom in the attic and, to be on the safe side, he wrote *4R* in pencil on the wooden headboard of his bed. Fourth from the Right. Not that he was likely to forget, but just to be sure. There, now that was done. What next? Oh yes, going with Uncle Ben to see Van de Bos.

Downstairs, he found Uncle Ben heading into the front room with an armful of sticks of last resort.

With a twinkle in his eye, Uncle Ben said, "Happy with my work, boss?"

"A first-class job," Michiel praised him. "Shall we go? You can probably borrow Father's bike."

"I've already asked him," replied Uncle Ben. "He said yes. So what kind of state is your bike in?"

"One rubber tyre and a wooden one," said Michiel cheerfully. "Bumpy, but it works."

"Jolly good. Then off we go."

On the way there, Uncle Ben told him about the underground resistance in Utrecht.

"Our most important job is organizing escape routes," he said.

"From prison? Isn't that impossible?"

"No, not from prison, although there have been some impressive cases of that too. Escape routes out of the country. British and American planes are shot down almost every day. If the pilots get out alive, they hide and attempt to contact the local underground movement. We do our best to send them to England, by smuggling them out of a harbour at night, or over land, through Spain."

A plane flew low overhead, making it impossible for them to hear each other for a moment. Then Uncle Ben continued: "Some resistance groups shoot German officers. It's so irresponsible. All that happens is that the Krauts take prisoners, random civilians, and shoot them dead, without any kind of trial."

Michiel nodded. One of the councillors in a nearby village had been killed like that, not so long ago.

"And does it often work, getting them out of the country?" he asked.

"Not always. Sadly they sometimes get caught on the way. Then they're sent to a prisoner-of-war camp. But if a Dutch civilian is found to be helping them, they're up against the wall, no questions asked. Only after they've been tortured until they've handed over all their contacts, of course. So you can see why we try to organize it so that the various links in the chain know as little as possible about one another."

"Are you in much danger yourself?"

"No, not really. My department forges documents. I'm in touch with a few people in hiding who are masters at forgery. If you ask me, they should go into counterfeit money after the war. They'd make a fortune," said Uncle Ben with a grin.

It wasn't easy to have a conversation above the rattling of Michiel's wooden wheel. And then they had to turn right, down a narrow bike path, which meant they could no longer cycle alongside each other. Michiel knew the way, so he went first.

Farmer Van de Bos was prepared to sell Uncle Ben half a sack of rye for a reasonable price. The farmers in the Veluwe didn't profit from others' misfortune during the war. Strictly speaking, it was illegal for farmers to sell anything directly to customers, as they were supposed to turn over their entire harvest to the farmers' union, which was, of course, controlled by the Germans. Van de Bos gave Uncle Ben a suspicious look, but he was with the mayor's son, and the mayor was one hundred per cent trustworthy, so he didn't hesitate for long.

"They're fine people, the local farmers," said Uncle Ben, as they cycled back.

"Hmm, yes," said Michiel. "They're good people now, eh? But before the war, I remember you city folk calling them stupid yokels and such like."

"Not me. I've always had a high opinion of farmers."

The rest of the day passed by uneventfully. There was some shooting in the distance, by the IJssel, but that was so normal that no one paid any attention. Michiel looked after the chickens and rabbits, took a letter to one of the councillors for his father (the telephones no longer worked) and helped a passing man whose handcart full of potatoes had collapsed. In short, he made himself useful. Deep inside, though, a vague feeling of "I wish it were

27

tomorrow already" was gnawing away at him. That was because of Dirk's raid. Not that it was so dangerous. Small raids were a regular occurrence, but even so...

Evening came and, as usual, the house filled with vague acquaintances. From nine to ten o'clock, there was a constant drone of aeroplanes in the sky. American bombers, on their way to Germany.

"That's going to cost the lives of yet more thousands of ordinary civilians," said Mrs Van Beusekom, with a sigh, but her husband and Erica and Michiel weren't too concerned.

"It's their own fault," said the mayor. "*They* started this awful war. *They* were the first to drop bombs on cities—Warsaw and Rotterdam. What goes around comes around."

"No. It's absolutely nothing to do with that little girl in Bremen who just got a piece of shrapnel in her leg," said Mrs Van Beusekom. "War is a terrible thing."

The image of a little girl with shrapnel in her leg—that reduced them to silence. The droning died away.

The carbide lamp gradually gave up the ghost too. Michiel went outside and peered over at the neighbours' house. He couldn't see or hear anything. *Dirk must have got home long ago*, he thought, trying to reassure himself. He was just about to go back inside when he heard a vehicle approaching. Instinctively, he drew back against the wall. It wasn't going quickly. It couldn't, not with those puny beams of light from the blacked-out headlights.

To his horror, Michiel heard it stop at the Knoppers' house. A torch flashed on. He pressed even more tightly against the wall. It sounded as if some men were walking up Dirk's garden path. Yes, he could hear them ringing away at the doorbell. And then a boot kicking at the door.

"*Aufmachen.*"

The Knoppers must have obeyed this order to open the door, as Michiel heard the timid voice of Dirk's father and some yelling in German that he couldn't understand. Then the soldiers went inside, and everything was silent.

This is bad. This is really bad, thought Michiel. *They must have caught Dirk, or maybe they just know he was involved in the raid.* His heart was pounding.

The back door opened a crack and Mr Van Beusekom called out quietly into the night: "Michiel, are you still in the shed?"

"I'm here," whispered Michiel, who was standing practically next to his father.

His father gasped.

"Sssh."

"What are you doing out here?"

"They're searching the Knoppers' place."

Michiel's father listened, but there was nothing to hear, just a dog barking in the distance.

"Where did you get that idea?"

"I just saw them go inside. They were kicking the door."

"I can't imagine Knopper would ever dare to take any action against the Germans. Besides, they've got German soldiers billeted there. Are they doing a house-to-house search, do you think?"

"No," said Michiel. "They drove straight to the Knoppers' place."

The mayor thought about it. "Is it Dirk they're after? But he's got a certificate of exemption from work in Germany, because he's needed here. Could he be in the resistance, do you think?"

Michiel had to bite the tip of his tongue to stop himself from telling his father about the rations office in Lagezande and about the letter he'd hidden. But he stood and waited in silence, as did his father, both of them deep in thought.

Finally, the Knoppers' door opened again. The men came out and walked to their car. As far as Michiel and his father could tell, they had no one with them. But in the dim light they saw Mrs Knopper standing in the doorway, and she was wailing: "Don't shoot him. Please don't shoot him. He's our only child." The car doors slammed and the men drove away.

"I'm going over there," said the mayor. "Will you tell your mother?"

"Yes, will do."

Michiel went back inside. The guests had gone to bed, but his mother was still tidying up in the kitchen by the light of a candle. He told her what they'd seen.

"I'll wait for Father to get back," he said.

"Fine," his mother replied. "But go and get ready for bed, eh?"

Michiel felt his way upstairs. As he walked up to the attic, he saw to his surprise that there was a faint light coming from his room.

"Don't be startled," said a voice. "It's just me."

It was Uncle Ben.

"What on earth are you doing in here?"

"I was just looking for an English dictionary," whispered Uncle Ben, "and I found one, on your bookshelf. I need to write a note to one of my contacts, but my English is a bit rusty around the edges. Ah, yes, there it is. *Dynamiet*. Of course, 'dynamite'. What an idiot. Thanks, Michiel. Goodnight."

"You can borrow the dictionary if you like. I don't need it now that I can't go to school. And my German dictionary's more use to me now, unfortunately."

"No need. But thanks anyway."

Uncle Ben disappeared into the front room on the first floor where he usually slept. Michiel put on his pyjamas and went to wait in the kitchen with his mother. It wasn't long before his father came back with a worried look on his face.

"Dirk supposedly took part in a raid on the rations office in Lagezande. Got caught, they said, and it seems that one of the other men was shot dead. They searched the Knoppers' place, not too thoroughly, as far as I could gather, but they didn't find anything. Knopper and his wife are really shaken up."

"I can imagine," sighed Mrs Van Beusekom. "What's going to happen to Dirk now?"

3

The letter nagged away inside Michiel's head all night long. Sometimes he dreamt, sometimes he was awake, but the letter was constantly on his mind. That piece of paper might be able to save Dirk. Who would want to be in Dirk's shoes now? Being a prisoner of the Germans was anyone's nightmare—particularly if they thought you knew something and they wanted to get it out of you.

I need to act as normally as possible tomorrow morning, thought Michiel. *No one can suspect that I'm doing anything out of the ordinary. No one can see that I'm going to Bertus van Gelder's. I'll have to be so careful.*

Michiel thought he hadn't slept a wink, so it was a surprise when morning came. He did all the usual jobs and it was about ten o'clock by the time he secretly took the letter from the nesting box. It wasn't all that secret though, as he had to chase away a broody chicken, which squawked and flapped as if he were trying to put it—sorry, her—on a spit for roasting. But it didn't really matter—a cackling chicken wasn't going to make anyone suspicious. He tucked the letter under his jumper and rode off on his bike. He had a long way to go, as Bertus lived at least five miles into the countryside.

He wouldn't get to Bertus's place that day, though, as he ran into all kinds of trouble. It all started with his solid rubber tyre, which came off the wheel. There was a big crack in it, so he couldn't just put it back on by himself. He headed off to the bicycle repairman. Who wasn't there. Then to a different repairman. No tyres in stock. Have to repair the old tyre. Got to finish another job first. An hour and a half. Sigh. Back on the bike.

Michiel was still on the main road when he saw a car coming. The villagers of De Vlank were used to paying very close attention when motorized vehicles were nearby, and for good reason, as we shall see. Almost as if the pilot had smelt the car, a plane came roaring through the sky. Michiel reacted immediately. He jumped off his bike and took a flying leap into one of the holes alongside the road that had been dug for this very purpose, large enough to shelter one person. The car stopped and two German soldiers ran for their lives towards a cluster of big trees. Just in time. The pilot dived and fired a burst with his machine guns. Ducking down, Michiel made himself as small as possible. For a moment, his heart stood still as he heard the bullets rattling on the road surface beside him. Then it was over. The sound died away. He peeped over the edge and saw that the car was on fire. The two soldiers were unharmed, but one of the cows in the meadow beside the road had been hit. The poor animal couldn't stand up and it was bellowing mournfully. Emerging from behind their tree, the soldiers looked at their burning car. Then they shrugged and walked off towards the village.

Michiel could feel the letter under his jumper. It seemed to weigh a ton. But the cow was bellowing away. He thought the field belonged to Puttestein, and he couldn't simply abandon the animal to its fate. So, off to Puttestein's farm. Where all the menfolk were out. Mrs Puttestein was the only one at home and she had a bad leg. Michiel discussed the situation with her and then, in a foul mood, he went off on his bike to tell the butcher. Trying to patch up the cow would, of course, be pointless.

And so the hours went by. It was ten past three by the time Michiel set off for Bertus's for the third time. He was barely halfway there when he overtook another cyclist. To his horror, he saw that it was Schafter.

"Well, well, if it isn't the mayor's boy, Michiel."

"Afternoon, Schafter."

"Where are you off to in such a hurry? Is there a fire somewhere?"

Schafter was not to be trusted. Everyone knew that. He hung around at the barracks, sometimes ate with the German soldiers in their mess, did odd jobs for them, and he was suspected of having reported the Jews who were caught at Van Hunen's place last year. They'd been transported to Germany. As was Van Hunen. No one had heard anything from them since. And so Michiel quickly

34

replied, "I have to go and see Councillor Van Kleiweg in Lagezande."

"Well, that's handy. That's where I'm going. We can cycle there together."

Deep inside, Michiel muttered all the nasty words he knew. Look where all his efforts had got him. Now he had to go to Lagezande instead of to Bertus's. And what on earth could he say to Van Kleiweg? Michiel wasn't entirely sure that the councillor could be trusted either. As Schafter rattled on about this and that, Michiel racked his brains to come up with a good excuse for not going to Lagezande after all. He drew a blank.

"Did you hear about that raid on the rations office in Lagezande yesterday evening?" asked Schafter.

"Yes. People were talking about it this morning," said Michiel suspiciously.

"'People'? Who exactly?"

"Oh, I don't know. Some visitors, or something."

"So your father's sent you with a message for Councillor Van Kleiweg, has he?"

"No, I'm off to play poker with him. What do you think?" snapped Michiel.

"Hey, I was just asking," said Schafter, not at all put off by Michiel's tone.

A quarter of an hour later, they arrived at the house of the councillor, who answered the door himself and greeted them with a friendly smile. "Come on in," he said.

35

"No, thank you," Michiel replied. "My father just sent me to tell you that the waterworks meeting is on Tuesday next week, at the usual time."

"Oh, thank you, Michiel. Tuesday at four. Tell your father I'll be there."

"Will do. Bye, then."

"I just need five minutes here," said Schafter. "If you wait a moment, I'll ride back with you."

But Michiel wasn't in the mood for more of Schafter's questions.

"Sorry," he said. "I'm in a real hurry. Another time I'd be happy to."

As fast as he could, he rode back to De Vlank. The letter was still rustling under his jumper. But he didn't dare to go straight to Bertus's now. First he had to straighten out his story about the waterworks meeting. He hadn't completely made it up, as he'd heard his father mention that there'd be a meeting next week. Once again he seriously considered telling his father the whole story.

No, he decided, *I won't say anything unless it's absolutely necessary. So that's just going to mean a bit more work.*

Luckily, his father was at home.

"Father, I need to go to Lagezande," said Michiel, lying shamelessly. "I heard you saying something this morning about a waterworks committee meeting, didn't I? Do you want me to give Councillor Van Kleiweg a message?"

"Oh, yes, please," the mayor replied in surprise. "Good thinking. Would you tell him that the meeting is next week on Wednesday, at the usual time?"

"At four?"

"Yes. Thanks, son."

"Bye."

"So why are you off to Lagezande?"

Michiel mumbled something about wanting to "buy a chicken for a woman from Amsterdam who's staying over at Thingy's place" before slipping out of his father's office. Good, now his father couldn't ask any more questions. It was annoying that he'd have to go back to Lagezande, though. He'd hoped that he'd got the right day. Waterworks meetings were usually on Tuesdays, he thought. Blast it, and he was only one day out. Hup, back on the bike. And, of course, he bumped into Schafter again on the way. The man looked puzzled, but Michiel just raised his hand and quickly cycled on.

Now that nosey parker is going to spend the rest of the day trying to figure out why I've been cycling back and forth, he thought. Well, the man wasn't a mind reader. But he had a keen pair of eyes in his head, and that was worth remembering.

Michiel told Van Kleiweg that he'd made a mistake and the meeting was on Wednesday. Then he quickly cycled home, so he'd be back before dark. Bertus would just have to wait until the next day. For safety's sake, he hid the letter in the nesting box again, hoping there was nothing urgent in it. Michiel felt absolutely terrible. Dirk was in prison, and Michiel hadn't even managed to carry out one simple task. All that cycling had worn him out too.

As usual, a bunch of strangers came trickling in. Uncle Ben had left, and Erica hogged the torch for half an hour to brush her stupid hair, and Jochem kept sniffing every couple of minutes and...

Ugh, what an awful day.

4

The next day, though, was even worse.

As early as possible, Michiel was out on his bike. This time he got to Bertus's farm without any problems. There was no sign of anyone out in the yard, just the dog on its chain, barking away as if its tail were on fire. Michiel went inside. No one there. Where were Bertus and his wife, Jannechien? All the doors were open, so someone must be around.

"Hello?" he yelled at the top of his voice. Bertus wouldn't hear him, but maybe Jannechien would.

He headed back outside. Wait a moment, was that the clanking of buckets he could hear coming from the barn? Yes, Jannechien was in the tumbledown barn, lugging a couple of buckets that looked too heavy for her. She'd been feeding the pigs.

"Hello, Jannechien."

"The mayor's lad Michiel! Have you brought news about Bertus?"

"About Bertus?"

She sighed and put down the buckets.

"Well, I thought maybe the mayor might know what they've done with him."

"Done with Bertus?"

"So you hadn't even heard that they took Bertus away yesterday?"

"Who? The Krauts?"

"Of course. Who else?"

"Why? What did he do?"

Little Jannechien actually stamped her foot in fury.

"Nothing. That's what he'd done. He was feeding the pigs, just like me now. They turned everything upside down and inside out. They even searched his clothes. But they found nothing. Nothing at all."

"But they still took him away?"

"Yes. The swines. I let Kees off his chain. He went straight for one of their throats. The others had to whack the daft beast with their rifle butts until he let go. It's a wonder they didn't shoot him dead."

Michiel felt perfectly miserable.

"Was this yesterday afternoon, Jannechien?"

"Yes, about half-past four."

Michiel thought about it. It had to be a coincidence. There was no way Schafter could have guessed. When had he seen him for the second time? Around four? So he couldn't have had anything to do with it.

"Hey, Jannechien, did you see if they went to any other farms? Or did they just have it in for you?"

"Just us, I think. They came driving straight here in those nasty trucks of theirs. And I'll tell you this, Michiel, if Bertus did anything—I don't know anything about it— but *if* he did something, then someone gave him away."

Michiel gasped. "How do you know?"

"Yesterday evening, after he'd gone, I was all shaken up, so I cycled over to my sister's, you know, the one who's married to Endik den Otter. They live up that way, on the corner of the main road and Driekusmanswegje."

"Yes, yes, I know who you mean."

"Well, I get there, in a complete state, like I said, and I tell them about Bertus being taken away, and my sister says, 'Goodness me, was that at about half-four? I saw them in two trucks, turning on to Driekusmanswegje. If I'd known they were going to your place!' 'Yes, what would you have done?' I asked. 'Well, I don't know. Nothing, I suppose,' she said."

"You said someone had given him away, Jannechien. What does that have to do with someone giving him away?"

"Oh yes, my sister said they stopped on the main road first, and one of the men was talking to someone from round here, and when they'd finished talking, they turned up Driekusmanswegje and headed straight to our place. And that man had shown them the way."

"Who was it, the man they were talking to?"

"Oh, what's his name again? That pasty-faced chap. Always going around on his bike."

"You mean Schafter?"

"That's it. Schafter. You know, people say he's no good."

Michiel didn't reply. Somehow he felt guilty, but how could Schafter have known anything? Even if he'd realized that the visit to Councillor Van Kleiweg was a sham, he still couldn't have known it was anything to do with Bertus. He had to get away, so that he could think about things more calmly.

"I need to get going, Jannechien. I hope they let Bertus go soon."

"Will you tell your father? Isn't there something he can do?"

"Of course I'll tell him. But, to be honest, I doubt there's much he can do about it. Bye, Jannechien. All the best."

Luckily, she hadn't asked Michiel why he'd come. He quickly cycled away.

After a while, he stopped and sat down and leant against a tree to think. He needed to get everything straight in his mind. Dirk had told him about the raid and given him a letter for Bertus. He'd hidden the letter. No one could possibly have seen it. The raid went wrong. One man was shot dead, one got away, Dirk was caught. Michiel tried to take the letter to Bertus the next morning but everything conspired to keep him away. He was such an idiot—he should just have walked when his tyre broke. Schafter could have realized that he was making up a story for Van Kleiweg, and then he saw him cycling towards Lagezande for the second time at four o'clock. At half-past four, Schafter showed two German trucks the way to Bertus's house. No, there couldn't be any connection.

Then Michiel realized what must have happened. Dirk must have cracked. They must have tortured him until he gave them Bertus's name. And Schafter had simply pointed out the way when they'd asked him where Bertus lived. Of course, that was what it must have been. He broke out in a cold sweat when he thought about what they must have done to Dirk to get the information out of him. Dirk wasn't the kind of man to blab everything he knew after just a bit of pressure.

And then another thought occurred to him, one that scared him even more. If Dirk had given them Bertus's name, then maybe he'd also told them that Michiel had a letter for Bertus. That was what the Krauts had been after, of course. The letter. They clearly thought it would have been delivered by half-past four. They didn't know Michiel was such a bungler. But that probably meant they were waiting for him at home. Then they'd catch both Michiel and the letter at the same time.

That couldn't be allowed to happen. Michiel took out the blank envelope. He would destroy it, rip it into a thousand tiny pieces and bury them in the sand. Should he read the letter first? No. Then he couldn't give anything away if they caught him. He had to get rid of the letter. Decisively, he ripped it in two. And then he tore the halves in two again.

Wait a moment. What if it said something really important? Something that urgently needed to be done? Of course it said something important. Why would Dirk have gone to the trouble of writing it otherwise? Bertus couldn't do whatever it said in the letter now. And so it dawned on Michiel that he would have to do it instead. What a terrifying thought.

For what must have been five minutes, he sat there with the four pieces of paper in his hands. If he read the letter, he would definitely be involved with the resistance. If he didn't read it... ah, but it was too late for that now. When he'd accepted the letter from Dirk, he'd signed on the dotted line.

He took the four pieces of the letter from what was left of the envelope, smoothed them out and pieced them back together. This is what it said:

If you're reading this, the Germans have got their hands on me. I'm writing to you because there's someone who needs help. Do you remember that dogfight above De Vlank, three weeks ago, when a British plane was shot down? The pilot jumped out with his parachute. The Germans looked for him, but couldn't find him. I had more luck, though, and managed to track him down. His leg and shoulder were injured, and I took him with me. The shoulder wound's been taken care of and a doctor put the leg in plaster. The next problem was finding somewhere to hide him. You remember that forestry work I did back in '41–'42? We planted a lot of young trees in Dagdaler Wood. So I dug out a hiding place there, under the ground. There are four plots of young trees, each about three acres. The hiding place is in the middle of the north-eastern section. The entrance is surrounded now by a thick clump of spruce saplings. If

you don't know it's there, it's impossible to find. Anyway,
that's where the pilot is hidden. I take food to him every
other day. He can't walk, so he's going to starve if you don't
take him anything. Be careful though. He has a gun and
he's very suspicious. Talking to him isn't easy, as he doesn't
speak any Dutch—and I'm afraid your English probably
isn't much better than mine. No one else knows about the
hiding place, so take care.   *WL.*

Michiel had no idea what "WL" might stand for. He read
the letter three times before tearing it into tiny pieces,
which he buried under a slab of moss. Even though his
stomach was in a knot, he suddenly felt perfectly calm.
Alright, so now he had a British pilot to take care of.
That kind of thing could earn you the death penalty. The
question was: how much had Dirk given away? As little as
possible, he was sure of that. Maybe he'd only given them
Bertus's name and said nothing about Michiel. He had
to go home, carefully, and try to find out if the Germans
had come for him. No, wait a moment, it was still early.
First he should go and visit the pilot. The man hadn't had
anything to eat yesterday and probably not the day before
either. Right, so he needed some food. From home? Not a
good idea. From the Van de Werfs, then. They liked him
there, and it wasn't far. He hopped onto his bike.

Mrs Van de Werf was cleaning the bakehouse. They'd used
it all summer, but since it had got colder, they were eating

45

inside the main farmhouse again. Now the bakehouse had to be cleaned and tidied up for the winter.

"Hello, Michiel," said Mrs Van de Werf.

"Hello, Mrs Van de Werf. Nice weather today, eh?"

"It certainly is! You're growing up fast, lad. You want to watch out that the Krauts don't nab you. How old are you now?"

"Almost sixteen."

"Yes, you take care. They got my nephew in Oosterwolde last week and sent him to Germany. To work in a factory, they said. He's seventeen, but still... They're taking them younger and younger."

"I'll try to keep out of their way."

"And what can I do for you? I imagine you're here for food again, eh?"

"Yes, please, if possible."

"So what would you like?"

"Would a bit of ham be asking too much?"

"Well, since it's you..."

They went inside together. There were some hams, pieces of bacon, and sausages hanging in the chimney. Mrs Van de Werf took a ham off the hook and cut some slices for Michiel.

"There you go."

"Thanks so much, Mrs Van de Werf."

Michiel paid and was about to leave.

"Would you like a bit of bread and cheese?"

"Well, I wouldn't say no," replied Michiel.

46

She cut and buttered two thick slices of bread, slipped some cheese between them, and presented the sandwich to Michiel, a treat for which someone in Amsterdam would gladly have paid a fortune.

"Thanks, I'll eat it on the way home," said Michiel. "I really should get going."

"Run along, then. Bye, Michiel."

Once he was out of sight of the farmhouse, Michiel opened up the paper that was wrapped around the ham and packed up the sandwich too. Then he set course for Dagdaler Wood.

The north-eastern section. It wouldn't be hard to find. The problem was not being seen. When he was nearby, he hid his bike in the bushes and continued on foot. The wood was motionless in the autumn sunshine. Not a leaf moved. No woodcutters' axes penetrated the silence. There were no cars, so there was no sound of traffic. Only a few twittering birds revealed their presence.

Michiel looked around cautiously as he approached the young trees. How on earth was he going to get through there? The spruce saplings were tightly packed together, so tightly that at first he had no idea how to get to the middle. Wait a moment, there were fewer branches close to the ground. He'd have to try crawling between the trunks.

It was hard work and his arms and face were soon covered in scratches. From time to time, he stood up, looked around to make sure he was alone, and corrected his course. He was making progress, but it was slow. As far as he could tell, he was almost at the middle of the plot now. So where on earth was this hiding place? Warily, he crept onwards. But no matter how much care he took, the twigs still cracked underfoot.

"Don't move!"

Michiel froze. The voice came from nearby. Quietly, he whispered, in English, "I'm a friend."

He didn't know why he'd said that. He must have read it somewhere, maybe in one of those books about cowboys and Indians.

"Who are you?" the man said.

Michiel knew what that meant. He'd studied English at school.

"Dirk's friend," he said.

"Where's Dirk?"

"In prison."

"Come closer," the Englishman told him, and Michiel did as he was told, crawling towards the voice.

Before long, he noticed a tunnel sloping down into the ground. Against the wall leant a man in his early twenties. He was wearing uniform trousers, with one leg cut away to accommodate the plaster that encased his whole leg. His right arm was in a sling, and his jacket was draped around his shoulders. He had a wild beard, and he was holding a gun in his left hand. Waving the gun, he motioned for Michiel to go inside.

It was dark, but once Michiel's eyes became used to it, there was enough light coming in through the entrance for him to see how the hideout had been built. Dirk had first dug a deep, wide hole, then placed beams of wood along the sides to prevent collapse. He'd laid a large wooden sheet across the top, probably a shed wall or something similar. On top of that, there was some soil with a few puny spruces growing in it. There didn't seem to be enough earth for them to take root properly.

The cave was around seven feet by ten and just over six feet high. Dirk had done a good job, but the thought of spending all day and night in there, and with those injuries too... There was a heap of dry leaves and a couple of horse blankets along the more sheltered wall. Michiel saw a water bottle, a mug, an old woollen scarf, and that was all. My goodness, had the man really been living here for weeks?

With some difficulty, they began a conversation. The pilot realized he would have to speak slowly, and Michiel racked his brains to remember as much as possible of the English he had learnt at school. They muddled through. The pilot, whose name was Jack, was delighted finally to have a proper conversation with someone. Talking to Dirk, who hadn't really opened a book since he'd left school, had been a challenge. When he heard that Dirk had been caught in a raid and might have given away his secrets, he became very concerned, though. About Dirk, and for his own safety. Had Dirk told them about the hideout?

Anxious or not, he wolfed down the ham. He didn't have a drop of water left, and Michiel realized he should have brought him something to drink. It hadn't even occurred to him.

Jack asked if Michiel could come back the next day with more food and something to drink.

"OK," said Michiel. *That's assuming I'm not sharing a prison cell with Dirk tomorrow*, he thought to himself, but he didn't say anything, partly because it was too complicated in English.

The pilot showed him the "path"—well, the route that Dirk usually crawled along—which made leaving the plot of spruce trees a little easier.

"Be as cunning as a snake," Michiel had learnt at Sunday school. So he carefully looked all around before fishing his bike out of the bushes. So he made sure no one saw him leaving the woods. And so he didn't go straight home, but went first to visit the Knoppers. Mr and Mrs Knopper were still really upset, of course. He told them how sorry he was about Dirk.

Bringing the conversation around to house searches proved easy enough. In fact, they didn't talk about anything else.

"Did the Germans search any other houses in the village today?" asked Michiel.

"Not that I know of," said Mr Knopper.

"I'm always afraid they'll come for my father," said Michiel.

"Yes, I can imagine. Now that our Dirk..." He started talking about his own miserable situation again—which was only understandable, of course.

Michiel was fairly certain by now that the Germans hadn't been to his house that day. The neighbours would definitely have known. Even so, he felt nervous when he put his bike in the shed and went into the kitchen through the back door. But his mother just said, "Hello, Michiel. What have you been up to all day, son?"

So everything was alright for now.

"Nothing special. A bit of this and that," he said.

His mother was satisfied with his empty response.

The evening went by. Michiel felt an almost irresistible urge to confide in someone—his father, or his mother, or Uncle Ben—but he withstood the temptation. "A good resistance fighter is lonely," he'd once heard his father say. "He's alone with his task and his secrets." Michiel was well aware that he was now involved in grown-up work; there were lives at stake. Well, he'd always hated being treated like a child—so he would act like a man. And so he said nothing. Even though he kept expecting his mother to notice the worried look on his face and, at any moment, to say, "Michiel, what on earth are you fretting about?" And even though he thought every sound he heard was a German military vehicle. And even though he wondered how on earth he would get hold of food for Jack in the coming weeks—he still said nothing.

5

It certainly wasn't easy, though. Michiel went to see Jack the pilot every other day. He had to come up with countless excuses to get his hands on food. Not to mention all the reasons for his frequent absences. As the mayor's son, it wasn't too hard for him to buy food from the local farmers. He didn't even mind that it made such a big dent in his savings, which he'd earned over the past year by doing various chores. After all, it was for a good cause, and everyone said money wouldn't be worth much after the war anyway. The problem was that his parents mustn't hear from someone else that he was buying food and not bringing it home. To be on the safe side, he sometimes managed to find a few extra bits and pieces and take them home. He also made sure he went to the more distant farms, buying from farmers who didn't have much to do with the village.

All told, it was quite a job. But Michiel was delighted that the Germans hadn't come for him. So it seemed Dirk hadn't given his name away. Michiel was grateful to him for that. Maybe, he thought, Dirk had given them Bertus's name because he had nothing to hide, so they wouldn't find anything at his place. That meant he would eventually be released. *So Dirk must be counting on me to keep Jack alive*, he thought proudly. Oh no, that wasn't right. As far as Dirk knew, Michiel had taken the letter straight to Bertus. Had Dirk caved in so quickly because he thought that then they'd come for Bertus before Michiel had delivered the letter? Deep down, Michiel thought it was cowardly of Dirk to give in that soon, but he tried to push that thought away. What would he have done himself if they'd knocked out his teeth—or worse?

Jack wasn't the easiest of patients either. He was bored and he was also worried that the wound in his shoulder wasn't healing more quickly. The circumstances were far from ideal, of course. That cold, draughty hideout, with a heap of leaves for a bed—no government inspector would have given this hospital a glowing report.

Michiel did what he could to help. To start with, he took a few English books from his father's bookshelf, ones that wouldn't be missed too soon. He didn't pay much attention to the subjects. So Jack was puzzled at first to receive a book about natural remedies in the previous century, with beautiful illustrations of various types of medical baths, and even a sealed envelope inside for students over the age of eighteen (containing anatomically correct illustrations of the parts of the body that help you to work out if your new baby is a boy or a girl—oh well, it had been published back in 1860), along with a book about steam-driven pumping stations, and—thank goodness!—a detective story by Agatha Christie, plus an essay about the internal combustion engine, and a few other odds and ends. Jack came to the conclusion that Mayor Van Beusekom must have a wide range of interests, and he read the books so often that he learnt them practically by heart, as he was thrilled finally to be able to read something in his own language again.

Michiel also tried to make life a little more comfortable for his "guest". There was no way he could carry a mattress to the hideout without being noticed, but he brought some more old blankets and even managed to take along a folding chair for Jack. As time went by, he also provided planks, nails and a hammer, and on a day when there were some woodcutters nearby and no one would notice a bit of extra noise, he cobbled together a door to close off the chilly entrance to the hideout. It was a shame Jack couldn't do this work himself as a distraction, but his wounded shoulder would not permit it.

In spite of all Michiel's efforts, though, Jack became depressed. His shoulder injury was getting worse rather than better. Just once, Michiel had been able to rustle up a roll of clean bandages from somewhere, and he and Jack, both equally incompetent, had patched up the wound. Michiel had been rather shocked at the sight of it. When it refused to heal and the dressing got dirtier and dirtier, he realized that the shoulder needed professional medical treatment. But how? He didn't entirely trust any of the doctors in De Vlank or the nearby villages. The district nurse? He didn't know her that well. Ah, nurse...! Why hadn't he thought of it sooner? His own dear, exasperating sister, Erica, had been a trainee nurse in Zwolle last year. That was all over now, of course, but she certainly knew more about nursing than Michiel did.

Could he trust Erica?

Of course he could trust her—what was he thinking? He was becoming so suspicious that he'd soon start wondering if his own mother was a German spy.

Would Erica want to help?

Would Jack want her to?

Was it a good idea to give away the location to Erica?

Was there some way he could take Jack from the hiding place for a short while?

Hey, but how had Jack actually got to the hideout in the first place, with his leg in plaster and his bashed-up arm? He asked the pilot.

"Don't remind me," he said with a wince. He told Michiel how Dirk had dragged him through the trees on his side, pulling him by his good leg, and said he'd rather be tortured by the Gestapo than go through that hell again.

That was just a bad joke, but the journey clearly hadn't been pleasant.

"The war will be over soon," said Michiel. "It's been going on in the Netherlands for exactly four and a half years and one day."

"Oh," said Jack. "And how many minutes?"

His Dutch was coming along nicely. Michiel had recently brought him a book by Philip Oppenheimer to add to his collection of reading material. They had an English copy of the book at home and also one that had been translated into Dutch, so he'd borrowed both books for Jack. In his fight against boredom, Jack was studying the books eagerly, although he'd given up on finding any useful natural remedies in the book about the healing powers of bathing.

"We need to bring in someone to look at your shoulder," said Michiel.

"We can't," said Jack firmly.

"We have to," stated Michiel even more firmly.

Jack shrugged, which was so painful that he blurted out a few words that were anything but firm.

"You see what I mean?" said Michiel.

Jack glowered at the grubby dressing.

"How do we do that? Bring doctor from... um... Deutsch army hospital?"

"My sister," said Michiel.

"Your sister?" said Jack, clearly thinking he'd misunderstood.

"Yes, my sister. She's a nurse."

He didn't add that Erica's medical experience didn't extend far beyond emptying chamber pots and inserting thermometers.

"You can trust her?"

Michiel looked offended. "Yes, of course," he said.

"I mean," Jack said, "can she carry the—what's the word?—responsibility?"

Michiel had to think about that for a moment. Could Erica handle the responsibility? All she ever seemed to do was giggle with her friends, which often descended into fits of helpless laughter that sent Michiel running for refuge. When she wasn't doing that, she was endlessly brushing her hair in front of the mirror. She did help their mother, though, he had to admit. And there was her work with the aid committee too. But real responsibility, like this? No, she wasn't cut out for it.

"Well then," said Jack, "it's not possible."

"Wait a moment," said Michiel. "If you don't wear that uniform jacket, but an ordinary overcoat that I'll bring along for you, and if you keep your gob shut, she won't work out that you're a Brit. And if I blindfold her before we reach the woods and when we leave, then it should be safe enough to risk it."

"My gob? What's a gob?"

"Your trap."

"What's a trap?"

"The thing you have to keep shut."

"Must be my ears," Jack decided. "When you talk, I shut my ears?"

Michiel laughed.

"Hey," said Jack, "your sister. She does exactly what you say? English sisters do not do what English brothers say."

"Yes. I think so," said Michiel, more casually than he felt.

*

Amazingly enough, Erica agreed to do it. Maybe just out of curiosity, but she said yes.

"A blindfold! Sounds like quite an adventure," she said, "but don't you think it'll look a bit strange if anyone sees me walking down the street in a blindfold?"

"I won't put it on until we're in the woods."

"But there's no need. When we're in the woods, I'll keep my eyes shut and we can walk arm in arm, as if we're a courting couple, and..."

"I'm not going out courting with my sister," said Michiel.

"I don't think you've ever been courting with anyone, have you?" said Erica. "But it doesn't matter. It's just pretending! Who's this patient anyway?"

"You're not allowed to know. I mean, there's no need for you to know. The more you know, the more dangerous it is. And you have to promise me you won't say a word to him."

Michiel's voice was serious.

He sounds so grown up, thought Erica. *He seems almost like a man now.*

"I promise," she said.

"Do you promise you'll keep your eyes closed in the woods too?"

"I swear on my honour."

She held up her hand as if taking an oath, but Michiel wasn't convinced. He'd seen Erica make promises so many times, with varying results. Well, he'd just have to risk it.

"Do you have any bandages?" he asked.

Erica nodded.

"Where from?"

"Oh, I have my sources."

"OK, you don't have to tell me everything—I don't tell you everything either."

The next morning, Michiel took a very old coat to the hideout, one that a hen had once hatched twelve chicks on. That afternoon, he and Erica set off for the woods. Michiel took the usual precautions, which had become a habit by now. They went the long way around, he paid close attention to who saw them, and he didn't head into the woods until he'd taken a good look around and made sure no one else was nearby. Erica thought it was excessive. What did it matter if someone saw them go into the woods? But then Michiel had always been more of a fusspot than her, so she left it up to him. He'd only ignore her objections anyway.

In the woods, they hid their bicycles in the undergrowth and continued on foot. Awkwardly, Michiel held out his arm for his sister.

In some ways, he seems more like he's forty, but in other ways he's like a ten-year-old, thought Erica. Her brother kept looking to check that she had her eyes closed. She did her best.

After a while, Michiel whispered, "Now get down. That's right, on your knees. You can open your eyes if you promise to look straight ahead, at me. I'll lead the way."

Crawling forward on their stomachs, the procession of two people plus two bags reached the hiding place. Michiel announced their approach with a poor imitation of a blackbird. The response was the song of a finch, which sounded just like the real thing.

When Jack saw Erica, he exclaimed in English, "Oh boy!" Which actually meant he was delighted to see a girl at long last.

Michiel gave Jack's good leg a warning kick, after which the pilot kept his mouth firmly shut. With her skilful hands, Erica began to undo the bandage. When Michiel had done the same a week before, Jack had yelped and groaned, but this time he didn't make a sound.

She must be really good, thought Michiel proudly. He didn't realize that a man doesn't like to complain in the presence of a pretty girl—and it had certainly never occurred to him that Erica might be a pretty girl.

Erica cleaned the wound with cotton wool, which she moistened with some transparent liquid from a bottle. Then she sprinkled a disinfectant powder on the raw wound and covered it with a piece of sterilized gauze. One clean bandage—and Jack looked great. Certainly much better than half an hour before. In fact, he seemed almost blissful and was clearly struggling to keep his mouth shut.

"How long has his leg been in that plaster?" asked Erica.

"Five weeks," said Michiel. "It has to stay on for another three."

Erica gave a professional nod.

"I'll take it off for him when it's time," she said. "The dressing needs replacing at least once a week too. I'll be back next week."

Jack nodded enthusiastically.

"Right. Forward march," said Michiel grumpily. He thought there was too much talking going on and he didn't like the idea of a visiting schedule either. He'd have to have a word with Erica later.

They set off and reached home without any hitches.

"Visiting him every week? That's out of the question," said Michiel.

"What did you say?" Erica replied vaguely.

"You're not going back there again."

"Why not? Didn't I do a good job?"

"Of course you did. But it's already risky enough that I have to go there regularly."

"Fine. You're the boss."

Michiel gave her a searching look.

For once, she had a serious expression on her face. She knew she'd done something worthwhile, something important. And she'd been stunned to find out that her "little baby brother", as she often teasingly called him, had been doing such dangerous things for some weeks. *He really is a man now*, she thought. Erica gave her brother's hand a squeeze and went to her room.

Sometimes having a sister isn't so bad, thought Michiel.

*

61

Having his wound treated improved not only Jack's physical condition, but also his state of mind. When Michiel went to see him two days later, he was unusually cheerful and declared that he felt as right as rain. There was only one thing still worrying him: his mum. You see, his mother lived in Nottingham and he was the only family she had left. Two sisters before him had died at birth, and it was all very sad. He'd only just made it himself, and could Michiel imagine how his mother had tried to protect him from every little gust of wind, as if he were some delicate little flower? That was why he'd volunteered for the air force—he'd had enough of being mollycoddled. Well, actually, there was another reason too.

"What was that?" asked Michiel.

Jack's Dutch failed him. Resorting to English, he said, "My father died at Dunkirk, at the beginning of the war, in 1940. He sailed across the Channel in a tiny little boat to bring soldiers back to England from France. You know, when the Krauts were racing across France and tens of thousands of British soldiers were caught in a trap."

Michiel nodded.

"Bomb hit the boat," said Jack. "Bull's eye. Never found a trace of it. I was devastated, but the grief almost destroyed my mother."

"And now she's worried about you."

"Worried? I bet she won't have slept a wink, she'll be wasting away, her hair will be completely grey... She'll be the most miserable wretch in all of England. They must have reported me as missing. That usually means you've bitten the dust, but sometimes a message comes to say that a missing person has been captured and is a prisoner of war."

"So your mother will be waiting on the doorstep of the post office every morning?"

"Well, messages generally come via the Red Cross, so it's their doorstep she'll be sitting on. But I can't bear to think of her worrying like that. Do you know of any way I could get a letter to her?"

Michiel gave a deep sigh. Looking after a pilot wasn't easy.

"I'll think about it," he said. "How did you like my sister?"

Jack clicked his tongue. "Jolly nice," he said. "And my shoulder feels a lot better now. Such a shame I wasn't allowed to speak to her."

"That's life in an occupied country for you," said Michiel philosophically. "Does His Majesty have any further requests?"

"No, this is the finest hotel in the world. Just my mother, if there's anything you can do..."

"I'll think about it," repeated Michiel.

Then he dropped down onto all fours and began the journey back through the trees.

Good heavens, how on earth was he going to get a letter to England? Obviously, since the occupation there'd been no postal service with Germany's enemies. He could try to contact the resistance, of course. He suspected that Dries Grotendorst had something to do with the underground, but he didn't want to confide in him. "A good resistance fighter is lonely. He's alone with his task and his secrets," he kept repeating to himself. But he couldn't get the image of Jack's mother going to the Red Cross every day out of his mind. What could he do? He knew of one possibility, but was it a good idea? It was the first thought that had come to mind when Jack mentioned the letter to England: Uncle Ben. He knew all about escape routes—so he must be able to get a letter into England, mustn't he? But still he wasn't keen on the idea of telling yet another person about Jack.

The pilot persisted, though, and eventually Michiel gave in and said, "Go on then. Write the letter. And make sure you don't say anything that could be a clue to where you are."

"OK," said Jack, and he wrote that he was alive and kicking and not in German hands and that he'd been slightly injured but not too badly, and that his mother had nothing to worry about, as "a fine young man" of six- teen was taking excellent care of him. Michiel was rather flattered by that last sentence, but it wasn't essential, so it had to be scrapped. He told Jack that, no matter how alive and kicking he was (although he wouldn't be doing much kicking with that plaster on his leg), all he could do for now was write out the letter again.

Two days later, Uncle Ben turned up at the Van Beusekoms' house, and Michiel asked him to go out for a walk with him. "You told me a while back about escape routes for British soldiers. So... would you be able to get a letter to England?"

Uncle Ben gave Michiel a searching look.

"What kind of letter?"

"You know, words on paper."

Uncle Ben smiled. But not for long. His expression became serious as he gripped Michiel's arm. "You're not telling me you're involved with the underground, are you?"

"No. It's just that there's a friend of a brother of a friend of mine who wants to get the letter sent. Can you help or not?"

"So who is this friend with a brother?"

"Right. Then you can't help," said Michiel, who definitely didn't want to be interrogated. "The weather's getting chilly, don't you think?"

"Well, well," said Uncle Ben, "you've certainly got what it takes, haven't you? Hand over the letter."

Michiel took it from his pocket.

"There you go."

"Thank you."

Not another word was spoken about the transaction.

"The letter is on its way," Michiel said to Jack. Then he gasped. "Your bandage has been changed!"

Jack nodded meekly.

"Erica?"

"Yes."

"The rotten liar. How did she manage to find you?"

"No idea," said Jack. "Probably she did not close her eyes last time. She thought I need new bandage but you not too happy. And so she come here on her... on her..."

"Own initiative," growled Michiel. "So you spoke to each other too?"

Jack gave him a guilty look.

"And she knows you're a pilot?"

"Sorry. She guesses. She's not silly, you know. My Dutch very good, but is possible that she hears a little accent..."

"Ah, just stop it. Every other word you say is as English as Queen Victoria. How on earth am I supposed to keep you safe like this? They'll be coming for you any day now. And they'll put Erica and me up against the wall—and probably our father too. Bang. Bang. Bang. Three–nil."

"Erica does not say nothing."

"No, she won't say anything. But she isn't careful. She doesn't make sure that no one sees her. She makes noise. She leaves tracks. If someone like Schafter spots her going into the woods, he'll immediately be suspicious."

"Who is Schafter?"

"Oh, never mind. A fan of the Germans. One of the many. Well, I'm going to give Erica a piece of my mind. Maybe we'll be lucky, and we'll get away with it."

"You say the letter is gone?"

"It's gone. Safely, I think. Right, I'm off. See you."

"Ta-ta."

Michiel did indeed give Erica a piece of his mind. In fact, he called her every name under the sun, but all in whispers, as their mother was in the room next door. You try shouting at someone when you're whispering. It's a bit like slamming the door in a fury, and then having to go back because you've forgotten your gloves—you end up looking just a little bit foolish. So Michiel's words didn't have much of an effect on his sister. She stared guiltily at the third button on her cardigan and swore—perhaps a little too easily—that she'd never do it again. And when Michiel paused for breath, she said the wound looked better and that was good, wasn't it? And, well, that was the end of the whispering.

Michiel just reminded her once again not to say anything to anyone, not even their own father, and that was that.

Another week or so went by without much happening, just the normal everyday events. And then Uncle Ben turned up again. This time he took Michiel for a walk and he said, "Do you ever see that friend of a brother of a friend of yours?"

Michiel was immediately on his guard.

"No," he said brusquely.

"Ah, that's a pity," said Uncle Ben. "I have a letter for him from his mother. So it can't be delivered then. What should I do with it? Do you know what, I'll just put it under this loose strip of bark. And then I'll be shot of it."

He walked over to a tree and slipped something under the bark. Then he turned around and walked back to the house without saying another word.

Flabbergasted, Michiel took the white envelope. There was nothing written on it. What on earth...? Was it really a letter for Jack? Well, of course it was possible... Yes, there was a chance that his uncle had written a return address on Jack's letter and this was the reply. He decided to go and visit Jack.

Taking even more care than usual, Michiel made his way to the hideout. What if there was just a blank piece of paper in the envelope and all of this was a trick to make him lead the way to Jack's hiding place? Was Uncle Ben trying to follow him right now? Ah, he was so suspicious. Uncle Ben was one of the good guys.

Yes, he certainly was. When Jack opened the envelope, his face lit up. There was a delighted letter from Jack's mother inside, saying that she'd imagined him dead a hundred times, and a snapshot of her standing at the garden gate. Michiel mentally doffed his cap to Uncle Ben, who had made it all happen—and so quickly too.

6

One November morning in 1944. A deathly hush filled the village. No planes would venture out into those dense, low clouds. There were barely any cars left. It had been gently raining all night long. Now it was almost dry, but water was still dripping from the soaking trees. Not a breath of wind blew. It was grey and gloomy, all around. The roads were gleaming and wet. A black cat ran shivering across the road and disappeared into a shed.

The village was in the grip of fear. Anyone who didn't absolutely have to leave the house stayed indoors. A lone woman in clogs dashed out to fetch a few forgotten, sodden pieces of clothing from the washing line. She looked around timidly before scurrying back inside as fast as her legs would carry her. No one knew where it had come from, but a rumour had stolen its way into the village that morning. Yesterday evening, maybe last night, a patrol in the woods had found the decaying body of a German soldier. They said he must have been dead around six weeks. The Germans had thought he'd deserted, or so rumour had it, but now they knew he'd been murdered.

What was going to happen? How would the Germans take revenge? There were terrible stories about retribution following attacks on German soldiers. But how true were they? What could the villagers do to defend themselves? Nothing. Everyone was keeping quiet. No one wanted to draw attention to themselves. Black clouds hung over the village, low and threatening. Fear crept all around, nestling into the streets, the gardens, the houses. The village waited, motionless, for what was to come.

At ten o'clock that morning, a truck had gone racing through De Vlank.

Yes, now they're brave enough to come out, thought many of the villagers, *now that the clouds are protecting them from the British Spitfires.*

Brakes screeching, the vehicle came to a stop in front of the town hall. Eight soldiers jumped out. With their big boots, they kicked open the door and went inside. It didn't take long. It was not eight men who came back out, but ten. Between the soldiers walked the mayor and the town clerk, their heads held high. The villagers saw them for just a moment. Then they were bundled into the truck and the doors closed behind them. And on it drove. To the vet. To the solicitor. To Schiltman, the wealthy farmer. To the headmaster. To the minister. Ten men were taken from their houses and transported to the barracks on the road to Zwolle. They were not permitted to take anything with them. Not a word was spoken about what awaited them. Their wives, who tried to protest, were roughly pushed aside. How long did the operation take? An hour? At most. The truck left and the silence of the village gave way to an anxious buzz of people talking, crying, speculating, consoling, encouraging, wandering in and out of one another's houses, hysterical and helpless, knowing there was nothing they could do.

The Germans had taken them hostage as an act of retaliation. Soon after the men were taken prisoner, the German commander of the local barracks announced that he would hang all ten of them the next morning from the trees on the village green, unless the perpetrator or perpetrators of the soldier's murder made themselves known before that time.

Erica was sick. She was literally heaving with fear. Mrs Van Beusekom had dark circles under her eyes. Her cheekbones seemed more prominent than usual and the right side of her mouth kept twitching nervously. But she didn't cry. She cleaned up Erica with a wet flannel and a towel. She gave Jochem, who had no idea what was going on, a fresh white sheet of pre-war paper and a pencil so that he could draw. Then she came to stand beside Michiel, who was sitting in a chair, staring silently into space.

"I'm going to go there," she said.

"Where? The barracks?"

"Yes. To see the commander. I've met him twice. He seems like a fairly reasonable man. I'll beg him not to commit this senseless murder."

"Shall I go?" asked Michiel.

"No, I think it's better if I do it."

Michiel knew she was right. Obviously his mother, as the mayor's wife, would make more of an impression than a young man of sixteen.

Mrs Van Beusekom put on her dark-blue suit. She powdered her face to conceal the circles under her eyes as well as she could, and then she left for the barracks. Full of admiration, Michiel watched her go. But what could *he* do to help? He had to think, think calmly. Who could have killed that soldier? Yes, how could he go about finding that out? It could have been someone from another village, poachers maybe, who had been taken by surprise and had panicked. Or someone from the resistance... But no, that was unthinkable. They weren't that foolish. Everyone knew that killing a German would only provoke retaliation from the *Wehrmacht*. There was a chance, though, that the underground knew something about it. But Michiel didn't know anyone who was in the resistance, except for Dirk and Bertus, and they were behind bars. But who else *might* be in the resistance? Michiel considered the men of the village, one by one. He was almost certain that Dries Grotendorst was a member. But Dries had always been a little reckless... Ah, Mr Postma the teacher! Yes, definitely. Michiel remembered the fourth year of primary school, when Mr Postma had spoken so passionately and patriotically about the Eighty Years' War and the Dutch longing for freedom. His father had once or twice jokingly remarked that the Dutch weren't the only ones with a need for freedom, but still... Mr Postma was sure to be in the resistance.

Michiel put on his ragged old coat and headed over there. Oh, he was such an idiot. Mr Postma was at school, of course. Then he would have to wait until lunchtime. When twelve o'clock came, Michiel met the teacher at his garden gate.

"Hello, sir," said Michiel sadly.

"Hello, Michiel."

His greeting didn't sound much happier than Michiel's. They both knew exactly what was on each other's mind: the mayor and the headmaster and the other eight men.

"You don't happen to know who killed that German, do you?" asked Michiel.

Mr Postma shook his head.

"And I don't suppose you know who's the head of the resistance in De Vlank?"

Again, Mr Postma shook his head, a little more slowly this time. Michiel gave him a hard stare.

"Well, if you should happen to meet him, will you pass on this message from me?"

Mr Postma didn't reply.

"Will you tell him that the perpetrator must hand himself in to the Germans today?"

Mr Postma gave him an almost imperceptible nod.

"I wish you and your mother strength in this difficult time," he said. "And now I really need to get going," he continued with a very small smile, which, with a healthy dose of imagination, could have been seen as conspiratorial. "Bye, Michiel."

"Bye, sir."

With a spark of hope the size of a glow-worm, Michiel walked home, where he found his mother sitting on a chair in the kitchen, doing nothing. The commander had refused to see her.

The day crept by. The weather remained miserable. The stream of people passing through was smaller than usual. Had word got around? Were people avoiding the village? Or was it the weather? Even so, hundreds still walked through the village that day. One old man was pulling a trolley, a sort of handcart on four wooden wheels, big enough for transporting a couple of toddlers. It wasn't carrying children now though, but a sack of potatoes. Right in front of the mayor's house, one of the wheels cracked in two. The old man was at a complete loss. He stood there, tugging at the cart, as if that might somehow repair the wheel. Finally he sat down on a post and gazed miserably into the distance.

Michiel walked over to him. He wasn't in the mood for helping, but he was so used to it by now that his legs walked there almost by themselves.

"Wheel's broken," he diagnosed.

The old man nodded.

"Shall we get it repaired then?"

The man looked up in surprise. That option didn't seem to have occurred to him.

"Is that... possible?" he asked hopefully.

"Maybe," said Michiel. "Wait there a moment."

He went to the shed to fetch some tools. Removing the broken wheel from the axle proved fairly easy.

"If you wait here, I'll take it to the repair shop. Alright?"

The old man nodded again. He didn't appear to be the sharpest knife in the drawer.

Michiel jumped onto his bike. The cartwright gave him a sympathetic smile when he walked into his workshop. As if there'd been a death in the family. He dropped all his other work to repair the wheel. Michiel thought it was almost creepy. The man was so obliging that it was as if Michiel had uttered a dying request.

Half an hour later, the wheel was ready. Michiel cycled back. Suddenly he realized he was riding across the village green. Seven large chestnut trees stood motionless in the drizzle. Enough thick branches to hang ten men from. But there was no way that could be allowed to happen. It was unthinkable that his father, his decent, clever, *kind* father would have a rope put around his neck and... It couldn't happen. It mustn't happen.

It could happen, Michiel knew. It had happened before—and for less.

He'd heard that they'd once hanged all the men in a French village from lampposts. And a story he'd been told by one of the people who'd stayed with them was still fresh in his mind. The SS had raided a house in Gouda, or in Woerden, somewhere in that part of the country. A father, mother and six children. They'd found some guns. So they took the whole family out into the garden and shot the father and the two eldest sons dead in front of the mother and the younger children.

Such things did happen, and more and more often as it became increasingly obvious that the Germans were going to lose the war. Michiel swallowed hard. Then he tore his eyes from the chestnut trees and went on his way.

He found the old man still sitting there on the post. A look of delight came onto his face when he saw that the wheel had been repaired.

"How on earth did you manage that?" he asked.

"With a few rivets and a new iron band."

"Incredible. How much do I owe you?"

"Three guilders."

"Here you go. And a couple of coins for your trouble."

Michiel couldn't help smiling at that. He'd earned a bit of money. Imagine if he started asking for payment for all the jobs he did for people. How much should he charge for looking after Jack? But he simply said thank you and put the money in his pocket.

"So, now you can be on your way again, sir."

The old man laid one hand on Michiel's arm.

"Those potatoes. They're for my daughter and her two little ones," he said. "I hope they're still alive when I get home."

"Where do you live?"

"In Haarlem."

Walking to Haarlem, with a handcart full of potatoes. That must be about eighty miles!

"Excuse me, sir, but how old are you?"

"I'm seventy-eight. God will reward you, my boy."

He took hold of the handle of his cart and trudged away. A ring of grey hair poked out from beneath his soaking-wet hat.

Michiel watched him go.

War is so cruel, he thought.

It can't have been easy for the ten prisoners that night, or indeed for their wives and children. The Van Beusekoms had only four guests. Two distant cousins, both spinsters around thirty, a former mayor who had also studied with Mr Van Beusekom, and an actual aunt. The guests could tell that they were intruding, and they kept as quiet as mice. Michiel lit the lamp for them and then went to fetch milk. Suddenly he realized with a shock that he'd completely forgotten to visit Jack. And he hadn't been the previous day either. Now it was too late. There was no way he could be back before eight and he didn't want to make his mother even more anxious. Oh, how frustrating.

To share his misery with someone, he whispered to Erica, "I forgot to go and see Jack."

"It's alright," said Erica quietly.

"What?"

"I went. I took him something to eat."

Blast it all, that Erica. She just did whatever she felt like doing.

"Did you tell him about Father?"

"No. He already has enough on his mind. His wound's playing up again. I tell you, Michiel, he's not looking at all well. That hole's too cold and damp for him to heal properly."

Michiel thought Erica's visits to the hideout were a huge risk. A girl going into the woods on a regular basis—people were sure to notice. But what could he do? It was his own fault. He was the one who had got her involved.

He couldn't dwell on the Jack problem for too long though. His other worry occupied his thoughts entirely. He looked at the clock: ten to nine. His mother couldn't sit still. She kept standing up to do some unimportant bit of housework—moving a vase or something else equally unnecessary. By quarter-past nine, all the guests were in bed. Erica, who had managed to be brave until then, began to cry quietly, her head on her mother's shoulder. Mother stroked Erica's hair; she didn't know what to say. Michiel broke sticks of last resort into pieces, smaller and smaller, and he had no idea what to say either.

"What time is it?"

"Quarter to ten."

Silence.

Erica got up and went to the kitchen to make another cup of ersatz coffee for everyone.

"I wish I was Jochem," said Michiel.

His little brother had been sleeping peacefully for hours.

"I can't imagine what your father must be going through," whispered Mrs Van Beusekom.

"Father and the nine others."

"Do you think he'll be praying?" asked Erica, handing Michiel his coffee.

Mother nodded slowly.

"I think even the most confirmed atheist would be praying in these circumstances. I know it's practically all I'm doing."

"Me too," said Erica.

Michiel said nothing. He hadn't even thought about praying. His head was full of all kinds of wild and impossible plans for rescuing his father. He imagined disguising himself in a German uniform to get inside the barracks. He would go straight to the commander and, holding a gun to the man's head, force him to telephone through the order for the prisoners' immediate release. Yes, if only—hey presto!—he had a German uniform and a revolver. And even then... Oh, it was all nonsense. There was nothing he could do. He wished Uncle Ben were around. Maybe he could come up with a plan. Could he track down Uncle Ben? Before tomorrow morning? Not likely. Not when being outside after eight was forbidden and there were no telephone lines, unless you were German, of course, and when no one ever knew where to find Uncle Ben anyway. No chance.

Should he pray? No, he wanted to actually *do* something! Did praying count as doing something? He looked at his mother and at Erica. Both of them sat with their hands in their laps, staring into the fire. He tried to calm his mind, tried to concentrate on what he'd learnt at Sunday school when he was younger. Was God listening to what Erica was asking Him? The trees on the village green stood between him and God. How would they do it? Would his father have to climb up onto a box, which they'd pull from under his feet? That couldn't happen. God couldn't allow it to happen. Or could God allow it? So should he be praying?

Michiel got up and went to stand by the back door, gazing up at the sky, which had cleared by now. The stars looked down, cold and distant. Then one of them fell.

"I want my father safely back home," Michiel said quickly. When a star fell, you were allowed to make a wish, weren't you?

What if that soldier had been hit by a falling tree? Or struck by lightning? Maybe he'd had a heart attack. Oh no, his head was bashed in. But it could have been a falling tree. Would the commander have considered that possibility? Michiel ran to his room, as quickly as he could in the dark. He lit a candle and looked for a piece of paper. In his best German (which wasn't very good), he wrote:

Dear Commander,

You have said that you will hang ten men tomorrow morning if it is not known by then who killed the German soldier. Could the soldier have been killed by a falling tree? I remember that there was a terrible thunderstorm about six weeks ago. Maybe the lightning hit a tree and the tree fell on the soldier.

Would you please consider giving us a little more time to investigate this possibility?

With the greatest respect,

Michiel van Beusekom

He put the letter in an envelope and slipped through the night to the Knoppers' house. The living-room window was blacked out with paper. Quietly, he tapped on the glass. The front door opened a crack, and Mrs Knopper whispered nervously: "Dirk?"

"No, no, it's me," said Michiel.

"Oh, it's you, is it?" said a disappointed voice. "For a moment I thought..."

"I'm sorry."

"No, lad. I know you're all terribly worried, just like us. What can I do for you?"

"I have a letter for the camp commander. You still have officers billeted here, don't you? Could you ask one of them if he'll deliver the letter for me?"

"I don't know," hesitated Mrs Knopper. "When does the commander need to have the letter?"

"Before tomorrow morning. Before they..."

"Give it here. I'll try. Wait here a moment."

She disappeared upstairs. Michiel heard voices in the distance and then she came back down.

"He'll do it. He's going to the barracks tomorrow at six."

"Thank you, Mrs Knopper. You've heard nothing from Dirk then?"

"Not a word."

"I'm sorry. Goodnight."

"Try to get some sleep if you can, Michiel."

"Where have you been?" Mrs Van Beusekom asked. Michiel told her what he'd done. His mother stroked his short hair.

"Let's hope it helps. Come on, we need to sleep."

"Sleep? As if," said Erica.

"Let's go and lie down for a bit anyway. If we don't sleep, then at least we'll get some rest." They went to their rooms. Half an hour later, all three of them were still lying awake in their beds, staring into the darkness with wide-open eyes.

The rumour must have come from Farmer Zwanenburg, whose house was right next to the barracks. He'd told the milkman, and the milkman had told a dozen other farmers on his round as he collected the milk churns from the farms. Before long the whole village knew. At half-past six that morning, shots had been heard at the barracks. A lot of shots, all at once, like an execution squad firing.

Michiel and his mother and Erica wandered anxiously around the house, their faces pale from the tension and the sleepless night. They'd heard the rumours too.

"I'm going back to the barracks," said Mrs Van Beusekom. "We need to know for sure."

That turned out not to be necessary.

At eight o'clock, before she set off, some soldiers posted a notice on the church wall. It said that four of the ten prisoners had been shot dead that morning. If the name of the soldier's murderer was not known by the following morning, the remaining six would be next. The four unfortunate men were the town clerk, the vet, the headmaster and a man from the city, who had come to live in De Vlank after he retired. Their wives received a letter at home, covered in official stamps. It confirmed their husbands' deaths in the correct and formal manner. The German army's administration was flawless. And that was not all. That afternoon the men's bodies were returned home in coffins.

It was as if a menacing growl could be heard throughout the village, a stifled scream of fury that might erupt at any moment. No Germans dared to walk the streets alone that day, and the collaborators and traitors didn't show their faces. Fear had paralysed the families of the six remaining hostages. They were so tired they could no longer think straight.

Every day passes—including that one, 23rd November 1944. Another sleepless night, with occasional brief periods of a kind of unconsciousness, brought about by exhaustion.

Michiel was up at half-past six. He raised the blackout blinds. It was barely light, but he could see the street. As he lit the stove, he occasionally glanced outside. What was that? A group of men was walking by, dark silhouettes in the dim light. The one at the front, walking with a stoop, wasn't that Schiltman, one of the ten prisoners?

Michiel raced outside. It *was* Schiltman and the solicitor and the tax inspector and, and... where was his father?

"Where's my father?" he yelled, grabbing Schiltman by the arm.

"Oh, you gave me a fright, lad. Who are you again?"

"That's Michiel, the mayor's son," Van de Hoeven, the solicitor, said hesitantly.

"The mayor's son?"

Why did Schiltman say it so quietly?

"Why isn't my father with you?" asked Michiel, his voice trembling.

"They shot him dead, not an hour ago. They let the five of us go home, but the murderers shot him dead."

Michiel let go of Schiltman's arm. Silently, he turned around and walked home. His mother and Erica had heard him shouting and came out to meet him, their eyes wide with fear.

The Germans must have thought that if they shot all six, the villagers might rebel. They'd seen the fury on people's faces the day before. So they sent five of the men home, to keep people calm. And to save face, they shot the mayor. They didn't trust him anyway. Then they could bring in a new mayor who was more to their liking. So the mayor happened to have a family, including a six-year-old son who would have to get by without a father now—but what did that matter? It was a war, after all.

7

It was about a week after the funeral. Michiel's eyes seemed a little more deeply set than before. Had he become thinner, or was he just clenching his jaw more tightly? There was a look of determination on his face. He felt a bit like the head of the family now, even though his mother was still alive and Erica was older than him. It was strange, but he was *less* afraid of the Germans than before. He'd resolved to do everything in his power to make sure this terrible war ended in a German defeat, as long as that didn't involve putting any lives at risk.

That meant no direct attacks on soldiers or on German property. That much was clear. But he would support anyone who was hunted and persecuted by the enemy. And so he was even more determined that Jack would survive the war—at least he would if Michiel had anything to do with it.

Anyway, it was about a week after his father's funeral and Michiel was visiting the hideout. As carefully as ever, he crept closer. But when the entrance came into sight, he didn't see the British pilot there as usual, looking keenly around, his pistol in his left hand. It was strange, but Jack always heard him coming, no matter how quiet he was.

"Psst," he said.

No answer. What was going on? Had Jack been caught? Was he heading into a trap? Carefully he peered inside. To his relief—and irritation—he saw Jack and Erica, blissfully unaware of the existence of the rest of the world, exchanging kisses.

"What's wrong, Erica?" Jack asked tenderly. "You look so pale and sad lately."

"Nothing, nothing," said Erica. "There's really nothing for you to worry about." And then she added, "But it's so sweet of you to ask."

The cuddling began again.

"Hm!" coughed Michiel. "Am I disturbing you?"

The two lovebirds leapt to their feet.

"Vigilance before romance," said Michiel, like a hardened veteran of war.

"I'm sorry," Jack said with a grin. "I've, um, grown rather fond of your sister."

"So it would seem," said Michiel. "You know, I think bringing Erica here was probably the most foolish thing I've done in this entire war."

"Why? Why shouldn't we spend time together? What have you got against him?"

"I don't have anything against him, you dope. I have something against you and him and me ending up the same way as Father."

"Your father?" asked Jack.

"He was shot last week in a reprisal," said Michiel.

87

Jack gasped. "Shot? Dead? Last week? What a nightmare. My poor love. That's why you're so sad." He hugged Erica against his uninjured left side.

Michiel was annoyed at the situation, but he'd seen enough couples in love to know that it would be easier to separate the Magdeburg hemispheres than to stop Erica coming to visit Jack.

"Fine then," he said. "But the very least you can do is bring Jack's food for him now and then."

Erica wasn't going to take that lying down.

"You little brat," she said. "You're talking to your big sister! You don't get to tell me what to do. It's the other way round, and don't you forget it."

"Looking after him is my responsibility," said Michiel calmly.

"It's true, sweetheart, as long as Dirk is in prison, your brother's in charge of this operation."

"OK," said Michiel, "you can visit twice a week and I'll come once, if you promise that you'll be really careful—no, if you do exactly as I say. Always take a different route into the woods, and always at a different time of day."

"I think you're being over-cautious, but fine, I'll do as you say."

"That's my girl," said Jack.

Then Jack and Erica looked at Michiel as if they were wondering if he had somewhere else to be, and Michiel didn't enjoy feeling like a gooseberry, so he dropped to the ground and began his crawl back through the undergrowth.

88

It was Sunday. The flow of people passing through De Vlank had come to a stop. Michiel sat in the bay window, looking out at the empty road. There hadn't been much talking in their home since that Thursday morning. No one was in the mood for conversation. Only Jochem was still chattering away. If you listened carefully, you could hear a low hum that was gradually growing louder. Here they came again, the bombers, on their way to drop their load of death and terror onto the German cities.

"Good," growled Michiel. "I hope they hit their targets."

"Just think of all those poor, innocent women and chil..." his mother began. Then she remembered a conversation about the same subject, when his father was still alive. "They started it," he had said. "It's their own fault." Did she feel that same need for revenge now, which made you harsh and indifferent to the suffering of women and children if those women and children were German? She wasn't sure.

"Hey, look over there," Michiel suddenly exclaimed.

They all went over to look out of the window. In the distance, half a mile or so away, the road was packed with people. It was like a procession of ants, marching closer and closer, making little incursions towards the garden gates. The gardens filled as the locals came out of the houses, wondering what was going on.

The procession was getting closer. The Van Beusekoms went outside too. And they saw men, *thousands* of men, walking towards them in rows of five or six. They were carrying suitcases and bags. Large numbers of German soldiers, their guns on their shoulders, swarmed around, guarding them. But they couldn't prevent the men from dashing to the garden gates and taking the food that the villagers were handing out.

"Those men are starving," said Mrs Van Beusekom. "Look at the way they're snatching at everything. Do you see that man there on the right, behind that tall one with the green scarf? He just picked up a piece of bread out of the mud and sank his teeth straight into it."

"Why are those men so hungry, Mummy?" Jochem asked.

"I don't know, son. Come on, let's bring out all the food we have in the house. We can go without eating for a day."

They ran into the kitchen, sliced all the bread in the bread bin, fetched apples from the loft, milk from the cellar, cut two large sausages into slices, as quickly as they could, and carried it all outside.

The procession was already passing their house by this point. When they saw the food, the men immediately flocked around them. In a flash, everything was gone.

"Where have you come from?" Michiel asked a boy who was no more than a year or two older than himself.

"From Rotterdam. A raid. They picked up all the men they could find. We're off to work in Germany, they say."

"Keep walking," a German yelled, and the boy was swallowed up by the crowd.

"How far do we have to go to the barracks?" asked an elderly man.

"A couple of miles."

"Really? Such a long way."

"But... that's not far, is it?"

"We've come from Rotterdam. Four days' walk, without any food. I can't keep going. I'm not going to make it. Stomach ulcer. Can't take another step."

But he did. Off he went, his wicker case in his hand. Some of the Rotterdammers escaped during that march through the village, darting behind trees, hiding behind the line of onlookers, diving into ditches.

Mr Koster, a retired forester who had been living in De Vlank for a long time, almost turned it into a game, grabbing suitcases out of the hands of passing Rotterdammers and growling at them, "Stand next to me and put on your doziest expression." The guards would then come up to him, as he was the one holding the suitcase.

"What? I live here!" Mr Koster would bark at them in German. "We have suitcases too, you know."

They had no time to stop and investigate, so they didn't pursue the matter. Mr Koster returned the suitcase to its owner and sent him into the house while he chose his next victim. Hmm, no, victim wasn't the right word... He was like a guardian angel to them, managing to save five men with his trick. Quite an achievement.

All those thousands of men and boys from Rotterdam, exhausted from the long march, passed through the village and disappeared into the barracks on the railway line to spend the night there.

That night, Michiel woke up because he thought he heard something in the house. Was it his imagination? It was quiet again now. No, wait, wasn't that someone quietly closing a door downstairs? Was someone up? It must be his mother or Erica, who had got out of bed for some reason. He turned onto his other side to go back to sleep. But he couldn't drift off. He could tell that something was going on. Was it burglars?

Purposefully, Michiel stepped onto the cold linoleum. Because that's what you do when you're the man of the house. Without making a sound, he hurried downstairs, missing out the third step from the bottom, because it creaked. He stopped and listened. Yes. There was a murmur of men's voices coming from the front room. Well, well. His heart thumping, but with no hesitation, he threw open the door.

Four candles lit the room. He saw two strangers, a young man and an older one. Michiel's mother was sitting on the floor, bandaging the older man's feet. Michiel could see at a glance that they were raw and bleeding. When the door opened, the men were clearly startled out of their wits. The younger man leapt to his feet and ran to the back door. The other man sat there frozen, unable to catch his breath.

"There's no need to panic, gentlemen," said Michiel's mother. "This is my son. He's no friend of the Germans."

"Absolutely not," said Michiel.

"These gentlemen, Michiel, escaped from the camp at the barracks tonight. They made their way to the village and took the risk of tapping on our window."

"I'm sorry. We were desperate," said the older man.

"It's fine," she replied. "I'm glad you came to us for help."

"But we're putting you in so much danger just by being here."

"Not really, I don't think. You're just forced labourers, aren't you? Not political prisoners?"

The men did not reply.

"You escaped? That can't have been easy," said Michiel.

"It wasn't so bad," said the young man. "There are too many prisoners and not enough guards. The camp isn't surrounded by barbed wire, just a fence. But our German friends have other ways to make escape unappealing. At the end of the afternoon, when we'd only just got there, a man climbed over the fence and ran away along the railway line. He was unlucky. Walked straight into a patrol. Do you know what they did? They gave him a shovel."

"A shove? They gave him a shove?"

"If only. No, I said 'shovel'. You know, a spade. They made him dig a hole, in the verge, just outside the camp. When it was finished, they ordered him to lie down beside the hole. We saw everything, from start to finish. It was... barbaric. The SS officer, who'd just been standing there watching all that time, took out his gun and shot him in the back of the neck, casually, as if he were swatting a

93

fly. Then he kicked him into the hole with his boot, and commanded two of us to fill it in. 'This is what we do to people who do not appreciate our hospitality,' he said. And he walked away, swishing his stick."

Mrs Van Beusekom wiped her eyes with the back of her hand.

"But you still decided to escape?" said Michiel.

"Yes. When it got dark. It was easy enough to climb over the fence," the younger man replied.

"Even for, um... I'm sorry, is he your father?"

"Yes, I am. Forgive us for not introducing ourselves. My name is..." He hesitated. "My name is De Groot, and this is my son, David."

"I'm Mrs Van Beusekom, and my son's name is Michiel."

"Pleased to meet you," said Mr De Groot.

"No, climbing the fence wasn't easy for my father," said David, picking up the thread again. "But he managed."

"That was a big risk you took," said Mrs Van Beusekom. "Was escaping so important to you that you were willing to put your lives on the line?"

Michiel looked closely at the two men. Both of them were on the short side, the son was dark-haired, the father grey. He thought he could detect a trace of an accent in the older man's voice.

Mrs Van Beusekom cleared away her plasters and bandages. "There, that should make things a little easier."

Then she turned to look at him. "Mr De Groot, excuse me for asking, but... are you Jewish?" she said.

Both men blushed. Michiel felt his cheeks turning red too. But yes, of course, she was right. That explained why they'd risked the dangerous escape. They had no choice. What would have happened to them if the Nazis had realized they were Jewish?

The older man looked helplessly at Mrs Van Beusekom. "S-so you could tell?" he stammered.

"It was more of a feeling," she replied.

He sighed. "Yes," he said. "We're Jewish. Our real name is Kleerkoper. Don't worry, we'll leave at once. We're putting you in real danger. Come on, David."

Both men stood up and walked to the door.

"And where exactly are you planning to go, Mr Kleerkoper?" Mrs Van Beusekom asked calmly.

"To Overijssel. We know a family there, who really are called De Groot. We can go into hiding with them."

"And how do you think you're going to get across the river? Every remaining bridge along the IJssel is closely guarded, and so are all the ferries."

"I don't know," said Mr Kleerkoper. "But we'll find a way somehow, David and I."

"Why don't you just sit back down? Four heads are better than two. But first, why don't you tell us how you came to be caught out on the streets? This is the fifth year of the war. Are there any Jews still walking around on the streets? I thought everyone who was Jewish was either in a concentration camp by now or hiding somewhere in a cellar or an attic."

"Well, it was an unfortunate combination of circumstances," said Mr Kleerkoper. "If you're interested, I'd be happy to tell you how it happened."

"Of course I'm interested," replied Mrs Van Beusekom. "The night's still young—it's only half-past three. And I'm all ears."

So Mr Kleerkoper sat down and told them the following sad tale.

The Story of the Kleerkoper Family

Jitzchak Kleerkoper was born in Germany in 1890. His name back then was Rosenthal, and he was a German citizen. He felt like a German too. Yes, it was true that he was Jewish, but that didn't feel like anything remarkable. There were Catholics and Protestants of various different persuasions, and he just so happened to be a Jew. In the First World War, from 1914 to 1918, he fought in the German army. One day, he found himself in a tight spot, but he bravely stood his ground and even saved a young officer's life. He was awarded the Iron Cross, Germany's most important military decoration.

Soon after the war ended, he met a Dutch girl. Lotte Kleerkoper was her name, and she came from a Jewish family too. They got married and, although they lived in Germany, she taught him how to speak Dutch. They had two children, David and Rosemarie.

In the 1930s, after Hitler came to power, the Jews in Germany were subjected to more and more insults and humiliation. The newspapers said that everything that went wrong was the fault of the Jews and that death was too good for them. Jitzchak became increasingly worried and bewildered as he saw all of this taking place.

Then, in 1938, Kristallnacht happened. That was a night when, all throughout Germany, Jewish people had their windows smashed, their property destroyed and their synagogues burnt to the ground. The Rosenthals had a furniture shop, and it wasn't spared: the windows were smashed, the upholstery slashed, the tabletops destroyed.

This event made Jitzchak decide to leave Germany for good—not because of the damage, not because it had happened, but because the German people, their neighbours and friends, did not protest. Because no one spoke out against it. "And that means there's no future for us in Germany," Jitzchak said, and he took his family to the Netherlands. He was so despondent about his fatherland that he gave up his German name and took his wife's Dutch name instead: Kleerkoper.

But then, on 10th May 1940, the Germans invaded the Netherlands too and immediately began tormenting and harassing Dutch people who happened to be Jewish. First they were not allowed to use public transport or to go to the cinema, and they had to wear a yellow star on their coats with the word "Jew" written on it. Later they were arrested and put in concentration camps—and finally they were murdered without mercy. Just slaughtered, like cattle in a slaughterhouse. In their thousands. In their millions. It's something you dare to speak of only in a whisper. Why were all those people killed? Because they were Jewish. That was the only reason. It's beyond comprehension.

Of course, many Jews tried to escape from the Germans by going into hiding. Jitzchak realized his family was in grave danger and he had made an arrangement with Mr Voerman, a good friend of the family's: they would all go and live in his attic. But it was too late. One Monday evening, when he and David had gone to the Voermans' place to go over the plan one last time, the Germans raided the house and took Lotte and Rosemarie. Jitzchak was under no illusion—the chances of ever seeing them again were almost non-existent. So it was only Jitzchak and David who ended up moving into Mr Voerman's attic. Jitzchak's hair had turned grey by then, as grey as ash.

About a week ago, the Voermans' house had been searched. The Germans had the cunning habit of arriving without warning at night, banging away at the door and then searching the house. Jitzchak Kleerkoper heard the thud of soldiers' boots below. He heard the familiar German snarls and the shaky voice of his friend, saying he had nothing to hide. He knew they would be found—there was no doubt about that. So he did something very daring. Putting on a dressing gown and some slippers, he stomped downstairs, yelling as he went. In perfect German. He'd fought as a German in the German army in the 1914–1918 war, so he knew all the military jargon.

"What is the meaning of all this commotion in the middle of the night?" he screamed. Didn't they know Colonel Von Brandenburg had a room in this house? That he'd been billeted here? Well, could they get it into their thick skulls that this was Colonel Von Brandenburg himself who was now standing in front of them?

By that time, he was in the front room and the officer who was in charge of the soldiers tried to say something. But the little man gave him no opportunity.

"Why did you not tell these people at once that I live here?" he barked at Mr Voerman.

"I'm so sorry, Herr Kolonel," the man replied in a weak voice. "I was confused. I'd only just got to sleep and these gentlemen woke me by ringing away at the doorbell and I—"

"This is a disgrace!" bellowed Jitzchak. "What is your name?"

The sergeant clicked his heels and said crisply, "Oberfeldwebel Maier, 3rd battalion."

"You have not heard the last of this, Herr Maier," growled Jitzchak Kleerkoper. "For now you are dismissed. *Heil Hitler.*"

Oberfeldwebel Maier clicked his heels again: "*Jawohl,* Herr Kolonel. *Heil Hitler.*"

He left with his men. Jitzchak Kleerkoper and Mr Voerman shook hands and said nothing for a while. They had narrowly avoided the concentration camp. The danger was over. For now.

"A magnificent performance, Jitzchak."

"Now you'll have to go into hiding too," said Jitzchak. "I'm so sorry. We'll need to leave first thing tomorrow morning, you and your wife and David and I. That Oberfeldwebel is sure to inquire about who exactly that unpleasant Colonel Von Brandenburg is. But how are we going to find new hiding places?"

Mr Voerman had contacts who were soon able to provide new addresses for them. He and his wife went to stay with the De Groot family in Overijssel. The journey would be too dangerous for the Kleerkopers though. "But if you happen to find yourself in that part of the country, then you must join us," said Mr Voerman. "They're farming folk with hearts of gold. I'm sure they'll find a place for you too."

Mr Kleerkoper and David were given an address in Kralingen, another neighbourhood in Rotterdam. Walking there was a risk too, but there was little chance of being stopped within such a short distance.

"Well, my friends, make sure you survive the war. I'm sorry you have to move on again. Farewell, until we meet again," said Mr Voerman when they parted company.

"Thank you for everything," said Jitzchak. "And as for moving on, I'd rather be a wandering Jew than a heel-clicking German. Good luck."

They went their separate ways. Jitzchak and his son walked straight into the middle of the raid. Luckily, the soldiers didn't ask for papers. They just picked up everyone they saw. The men were allowed to return home under escort to fetch a suitcase full of clothes. Jitzchak and David had no need. They were already carrying their belongings.

Then they'd been forced to march to De Vlank. They'd had no chance to run off along the way, as one of the guards kept a constant eye on them. Maybe he suspected something. So they hadn't been able to make an escape attempt until they were in the camp. Now they were free. But for how much longer?

"Until the end of the war, I hope," said Michiel's mother. "We'll have to come up with a watertight plan to get you across the IJssel."

"What if we disguise them? How about dressing them as farmers' wives from the Veluwe?" suggested Michiel. "They could wear the traditional costume. Put a white lace cap on them, big skirts, a bodice. That should do the trick."

"But that won't work at the IJssel. They check everyone's papers there."

"No, the disguise would just be for travelling along the roads," said Michiel. "We'll have to come up with something else for the IJssel. Wait a moment, I've just remembered something. The Koppel ferry..."

"What about it?"

"I recently heard an interesting story about it. And if it's true, we can get both gentlemen across to the other side with no problem. I'll investigate first thing tomorrow."

Mr Kleerkoper peered at him over the metal frames of his spectacles.

"Your son's certainly a plucky one," he said. "I'm sure you know the risk you're taking. But does he know too?"

Mrs Van Beusekom laid her hand on Michiel's arm.

"Until recently, Mr Kleerkoper," she said, "I didn't want my children to do anything that went against the occupiers' orders. I believed it was too dangerous and I also thought it was pointless. I have to confess that, deep down, I've always doubted that Michiel was following my wishes. For almost a year now, I've not been exactly sure what he's up to. Reluctantly, I resigned myself to it. But in times of war a boy of fifteen or sixteen is a man—don't you agree, Mr Kleerkoper? And besides, not that long ago, my opinion changed. I told you that my husband is dead, didn't I? Well, the fact is that the Germans shot him in a reprisal, without any form of trial."

Her voice didn't shake as she spoke those words, and no tears of emotion welled up in her eyes, but a flush of outrage coloured her cheeks as she continued, "Michiel and I have never actually said as much to each other, but I know that, since that day, both of us, and my daughter, Erica, too, would do anything to help put an end to their violence and murder. And so, my son, I'll gladly give you permission—no, in times like these a mother doesn't give her sixteen-year-old son permission. But I do agree that you must do whatever you can to keep these people out of the claws of the vultures who want to turn Europe into one big graveyard."

"Amen," said Mr Kleerkoper, bowing his head.

8

By the Koppel ferry, there was a large, white house. It belonged to Baroness Weddik Wansfeld, a lean and regal lady in her sixties. She lived in this house with her daughter and her son-in-law, her late husband's brother, two unmarried nieces, a butler and two maids. Even though there were a few men in the house, there could be no doubt about who was in charge: the dowager Louise Adelheid Mathilde, Baroness Weddik Wansfeld. People sometimes called her "Lamb" because of her initials, but only when she was nowhere to be seen. No nickname could have been more inappropriate, however, as the baroness was nothing like as sweet and gentle as a lamb.

The ferry was guarded, day and night, by five German soldiers, who were relieved every week. The commander of the garrison had ordered that these five men must be accommodated in the white house. The baroness had fiercely objected, throwing herself into the battle with all her might, and had even succeeded in making the commander come out to negotiate with her personally, but finally she'd had to surrender.

"Fine," she had said to the commander, in her impeccable

German. "They can come, but they must follow the rules of the house."

"Of course, Baroness," the commander had replied, with all the respect that German military men have for the nobility. "That goes without saying. Our soldiers are well disciplined and will behave most correctly. I will vouch for them myself."

And so the dowager had laid down her rules. For family and staff, there was just one rule: no one speaks to the soldiers except for the baroness. Even if it was merely about a broken cup, the baroness would deal with it herself.

A long list of rules applied to the soldiers though. They were not written down, because then the commander might have a chance to inspect them. Every Monday morning, just after the guard changed, the new men were admitted to the baroness's drawing room. She sat in a chair, her back as straight as a rod, while the soldiers stood politely at attention. Briskly and leaving no room for discussion, she listed the house rules. The sergeant would have a room in the house, while the privates would sleep in the coach houses. No noise after ten at night. All rubbish was to go in the bin in the pantry.

"From three until half-past, tea is served in the conservatory. Three o'clock sharp. I do not have sufficient staff to work in shifts. So I must insist that you all come together at three. The conservatory is large enough."

And on she went, listing more rules. So great was her authority—and the German soldiers' respect for that authority—that every new squad always fell for it. Tea from three until half-past. That was apparently the done thing. This meant that, from three until half-past every day, the ferry was not guarded. Only a few people knew about this fact. The news was passed on in whispers to trusted contacts. And every day Van Dijk the ferryman crossed the River IJssel between three and half-past with a boat full of people who would rather not be seen, who did not have valid papers, who wanted to smuggle something, and meanwhile Louise Adelheid Mathilde, Baroness Weddik Wansfeld sat in a straight-backed chair in the conservatory, conversing with the German *Wehrmacht*.

Early in the morning, at nine o'clock, Michiel was presented to the baroness. She received him graciously, offering her condolences on the death of his father and making no secret of her disgust for German methods.

"And what can I do for you, young man?"

"I'd like some information, please, Baroness. You live so close to the ferry. Could you tell me if it goes between three and half-past three? I'd like to take two farmers' wives across to the other side at around that time."

"I see. Two farmers' wives, eh?" the baroness echoed. "How old are you?"

"Sixteen, ma'am."

"Shouldn't you be at school?"

"There's no public transport to Zwolle now. And my bike's in no condition to—"

"I see. And so you're running farmers' wives around now. On the back of your bike?"

"I'm hoping I'll be able to borrow a horse and cart from Mr Coenen."

"And if not?"

Michiel didn't reply. What could he say?

"So why don't these farmers' wives go over the bridge?"

"Because... they prefer boats," replied Michiel hesitantly. He didn't want to give away any secrets, but neither did he want to be rude to the baroness.

"And why must it be between three and half-past?"

"I've heard that it's teatime then. They're hoping they might be able to have a cup on board."

"Who exactly are these women?"

"Um... what was their name again? Bartels, I think, yes, Bartels, Mrs Bartels and her daughter Aartje."

"And why are you taking them?"

"Someone has to. And besides, their surname begins with a B and so does mine. That... creates a sort of... bond, you know."

"Young man, I do hope you're not making fun of me."

"But, Baroness... why would I do that?"

A faint smile flashed across the baroness's lean face.

"Report to the cart shed at half-past one this afternoon. The carriage will be ready and waiting, with Caesar up front. I imagine you know how to handle a horse, don't you? The ferry leaves at five past three. I expect the carriage—and, more importantly, Caesar—to be returned by seven at the latest."

"Baroness, this is so kind, I—"

The tall woman had stood up, clearly considering the conversation to be over. With an aristocratic nod, she interrupted Michiel's stammered words of thanks. He quickly left the room, filled with admiration for this remarkable woman.

Jitzchak Kleerkoper and his son David shaved very carefully, and then used a little powder to conceal their grey stubble. The traditional Veluwe costumes were brought from the wardrobe of a local woman the Van Beusekoms knew well, and Erica and her mother made some quick alterations. The starched white caps helped to make the Kleerkopers look a little more like women. The two of them dressed up as farmers' wives—it was a comical sight.

"Catch," called Mrs Van Beusekom, suddenly throwing Mr Kleerkoper an apple. Instinctively Mr Kleerkoper clamped his knees together, the way men in trousers do when they have to catch something and they're sitting down.

"Wrong," said Mrs Van Beusekom with a smile. "A woman in a long, wide skirt automatically opens her knees outwards, like a net."

"Well, Father, looks like you've just had your first failure as a woman," grinned David.

"I'm a hopeless woman," Mr Kleerkoper admitted guiltily. "Maybe you'll be a better one, David."

He'd made a roll-up out of home-grown tobacco, which he flicked at David's lap. David, forewarned, opened his knees and caught the cigarette neatly in his skirt.

"Before you start looking around with that smug grin on your face," his father said, "let's see if you know how a woman strikes a match."

"I certainly do. A man strikes towards himself, with his middle finger just behind the head of the match—see, like this—but a woman holds the match higher and strikes away from herself."

He demonstrated how to light a cigarette in a most feminine manner, and then looked around triumphantly.

"I'm impressed," said Mr Kleerkoper, "although I have to admit I've never actually seen a farmer's wife from the Veluwe smoking a cigarette."

Everyone laughed, David the loudest of all.

"My father always has to have the last word," he said.

"Listen," said Michiel. "You mustn't say anything if there's the slightest chance that other people might overhear. Not just because you have men's voices but also because you don't know the local dialect. I have to be back on this side of the IJssel by seven at the latest. So there's enough time for me to take you farther than just across the river. Where do you need to go? Or would you rather not say?"

"The De Groots live in Den Hulst," said Mr Kleerkoper.

"That's about twelve miles past Zwolle," Michiel said. "We won't make it all the way there, but we should get a fair distance. Hmm. Let me think... if you have to walk the last four miles, you should be inside well before eight."

"We'd better leave right away, just to be on the safe side," said David.

"That won't help. We're getting the ferry at five past three."

"Isn't there an earlier one?"

"The crossing at five past three is the only one that's safe. When the war's over, I'll explain."

"I trust you completely," said Mr Kleerkoper.

At exactly half-past one, Michiel was at the cart shed by the white house on the IJssel. The carriage was ready and waiting, with the fiery black Caesar impatiently stamping sparks from the cobbles. Michiel felt anxious, but once he had the reins in his hand, his nerves changed into high spirits. The horse took off at a brisk trot, responding beautifully to each signal from the reins and giving every impression of being able to win the national harness-racing championships without any further training.

Michiel often worked with horses when he helped the farmers on their land. It was usually slow work because they had to pull heavy carts. But this was wonderful.

Later, once his two fake farmers' wives were in the carriage, he felt like a hero, a kind of Ben Hur. That feeling only grew stronger when, startled by the pace, Mr Kleerkoper anxiously clutched the seat and David remarked admiringly that Michiel clearly had a lot of experience with horses.

Sadly, his pleasure was short-lived as, before long, they passed Schafter. The man was on foot and as the carriage raced past, he held out his hand for a ride. Michiel had no more than a couple of seconds to decide.

Schafter up here with me, asking questions, no thanks, he thought.

So he pretended not to see the man. Out of the corner of his eye, he saw Schafter looking at his passengers with a puzzled expression, probably wondering why he didn't know who the two women were, even though he knew everyone for miles around. He was likely trying to work out where the mayor's boy Michiel was taking the women to. To the ferry, of course, that was where the road led, and Schafter wasn't born yesterday.

Oh well, thought Michiel, *he'll never reach the ferry before five past three if he's on foot. So it doesn't really matter. I'll just come up with some excuse to tell him later.*

Everything went smoothly. The crossing was uneventful. There was not a German to be seen. Michiel asked Van Dijk the ferryman if he could come back across at half-past six, and Van Dijk said yes.

"That horse there... It's the baroness's, isn't it?" said Van Dijk.

Michiel nodded. He expected the man to ask for an explanation, but Van Dijk had clearly decided to keep his own counsel.

They encountered no problems on the other side of the IJssel either, and drove for over an hour at a good pace. Then Michiel said, "I'd like to turn around here. I need to allow myself a bit of time, because you never know. And I think Caesar would like to go a little more slowly too. Will you be able find your way from here?"

"Certainly," said Mr Kleerkoper.

He and David climbed down and both shook Michiel's hand.

"God will reward you," said Mr Kleerkoper, using the same words as the old man with the broken wheel. What else was there to say?

"Now that we're going, it should make things a lot safer for you," said David. "I hope we'll meet again, Michiel. Farewell."

Michiel turned the carriage. He agreed with David, and thought that nothing much could go wrong on the return journey—but he was wrong about that.

Michiel had been driving for around twenty minutes when he spotted another horse and cart approaching along a track to the right. It was an ordinary flat cart, which the farmers used to carry hay and rye, but what was unusual about this one was that a couple of armed German soldiers were sitting up front—and there were *four horses tied to the back*. Michiel knew what that meant: these teams were sent out to round up and confiscate any horses they could find. About fifty yards behind Michiel, the German cart turned onto the road. By then, Michiel had already cracked his whip. Luckily, Caesar still had some energy left and he raced onwards.

"Halt! Stop at once!" Michiel heard them yelling.

What should he do? He looked back and saw that the German driver was also using the whip. Should he stop? That meant the baroness would lose her horse. If she was lucky, she'd receive a note saying that the German Reich owed her a horse. That wasn't much good to anyone. Besides, they might well question him. Ask him what he was doing in the area. He could feel the nerves in his stomach, but at the same time a look of anger and determination flashed across his face, a look that had appeared for the first time when he was standing by his father's grave.

"Faster, Caesar!"

Again, he heard shouting from behind. The Germans realized they were losing him. Their chestnut mare couldn't compete with that fiery black horse. But that was all the more reason for them to want it. One of the soldiers picked up his gun and fired into the air, startling Michiel. He wasn't far enough ahead to be out of the range of their bullets. Then he noticed a side road coming up on the left. At full tilt, he steered Caesar that way, so quickly that the carriage almost overturned. It was a track through the trees, clearly used by lots of horses and carts. Left and then right. Would he be able to shake off his pursuers? Ah, he could see now why so many carts had passed this way. The villagers had been felling trees and using the carts to transport the wood back home. He could still hear the furious cries of the soldiers behind him, but he could no longer see them. To the left, and left again... To his horror, he realized it was a dead end, and turning around was impossible.

"Whoa, Caesar."

Michiel jumped down. He tied the horse to a tree and fled into the undergrowth. If they caught him now, he didn't think much of his chances. He followed a narrow path. Was that voices he could hear? Yes, there must be people nearby. He decided to take a look. If they seemed trustworthy, maybe he could ask them if they knew of somewhere he could hide. But he had to be careful—you could never tell for certain if someone was to be trusted. Dropping to his knees, he crawled closer. His caution was wise. The voices belonged to his pursuers, who were talking to two woodcutters. Typical Saxon country folk, with blue caps on their heads and wads of tobacco in their mouths. Slowly chewing away, they took their time to answer the soldiers' questions, spitting out jets of tobacco juice, scratching their heads, gazing up at the sky wearing their doziest expressions; in short, they gave the angry Germans the impression that they were barely more intelligent than the average pig.

"So did you see him or not?" one of the Germans shouted.

"Well, there was a black horse that just went by, eh, Driekus?" said one of the men.

"It was a black horse, to be sure," said the other.

"And the cart, a carriage you meant, was it?"

"Probably," said the German, clearly irritated. "Just tell me which way the cart went."

"Oh, is that what you were wanting to know? Well... He went over that way, to the right." He pointed convincingly in the opposite direction to the one Michiel had taken.

The Germans gave him a suspicious look. Was the man telling the truth?

He smiled with the innocence of a little boy.

"Yes, that's right," said Driekus slowly. "That way."

"Thank you," shouted the German. "Forward, men."

They disappeared in the direction he had pointed. Michiel dashed to the horse, led him backwards down the path, jumped up front and quickly drove back the way he'd come. When he came to the two woodcutters, he stopped for a moment.

"So you sent them the wrong way?" he called.

The men grinned. One of them, the one who was not called Driekus, jerked his thumb over his shoulder in the direction Michiel's pursuers had taken.

"Yep. Following a black horse," he said.

"Thanks. So long."

"Bye."

A few minutes later, Michiel was back on the main road and on his way to the ferry again. He made it there just before half-past six. Van Dijk took him across and he returned the horse and the carriage to the white house. He would have liked to thank the baroness, but there was no sign of her. Then he cycled quickly home.

As he walked up the garden path, he thought he glimpsed his mother watching from the window. She clearly didn't want him to know she was worried, though, because when he came in she was working in the kitchen and she calmly asked if everything had gone well.

"Fine," said Michiel. "But on the way back, I got chased by some of our friends, who wanted to take the horse. They even fired a couple of shots. Just in the air though," he added quickly when he saw the fear in his mother's eyes. "Escaping was no trouble at all. That Caesar is a magnificent horse."

"That's good," said his mother, making a heroic attempt to seem unconcerned. "I'll make you something to eat."

But she couldn't help giving him a quick kiss on the back of his head as she walked past.

Just a couple of minutes before eight, Uncle Ben turned up. He hadn't visited for a while and so he hadn't heard about the death of Michiel's father. He'd always liked the mayor, and the news hit him hard.

"If only I'd been here," he groaned. "Maybe I could have done something."

"Like what?" asked Michiel.

"An attack on the barracks or... Oh, no, what am I saying? I'm sure there's nothing I could have done to help. So have they found out who killed that German in the woods?"

"No, of course not. That coward's not going to show his face. He'd rather let five innocent civilians get shot dead."

Uncle Ben sighed. "How awful," he said.

To cheer up his uncle a little, Michiel told him about Mr Kleerkoper and his son and their successful escape, and how he'd taken them across the IJssel, and the chase with the German soldiers who were after the horse.

Uncle Ben slapped Michiel on the shoulder, a little harder than was comfortable.

"Good work, lad," he said. "If the war goes on for another year or two, you'll be able to join the underground too."

Michiel only just managed not to tell him that he was already up to his neck in secrets.

In the middle of the night he was woken up by Rinus de Raat. The plane raced low over the house, two, three times. It was the kind of noise that made your heart stop for a moment and all your muscles tense up so that you could quickly sprint away.

Rinus de Raat was the village cobbler's son. Right at the beginning of the war, he'd run off to England. His father said he'd become a Spitfire pilot. So, of course, whenever a

British plane flew over the village, people always chuckled and said, "Hey, look, it's Rinus de Raat come to visit."

Michiel couldn't get back to sleep. He was thinking about Schafter. What could he tell the man? Because he was sure the clever and curious Schafter wouldn't rest until he'd got it all figured out, or at least thought he had. He didn't fall asleep again until he'd come up with a plausible story.

By then, "Rinus de Raat" had long since returned to an airfield in the south of the Netherlands, which had been in the liberators' hands since that summer.

9

The next morning Michiel decided to go for a wander past Schafter's house. Maybe he'd bump into him.

On his way there, he saw Mr Postma, the teacher. His first instinct was to look away. He was sure Mr Postma was a member of the resistance group in De Vlank, and weren't they responsible for five men being shot dead?

Mr Postma noticed Michiel's involuntary reaction and headed straight for him. He took hold of his arm and said, "I know I'm overstepping my bounds here, Michiel, but I just wanted to tell you this: the resistance in De Vlank knows nothing about that dead soldier in the woods. I'm absolutely certain of that."

"Thank you, sir," he said, feeling rather ashamed.

"Now, will you forget I told you that?"

"I've already forgotten."

"Good."

They both went on their way. Michiel walked past Schafter's house. He saw nothing. But then he walked on for a while and turned back to go past the house again, and he spotted Schafter working in the garden.

"Morning, Schafter."

"Ah, hello, Michiel. Were you trying to avoid me yesterday?"

"Avoid you? What do you mean?"

"On the road to the ferry. You went racing past in Baroness Weddik Wansfeld's carriage. That *was* the baroness's carriage, wasn't it?"

"Yes, it was."

"I wouldn't have minded a lift, but apparently you didn't see me."

"Really? I'm sorry."

"Doesn't matter. I was going to Verheul's. It's not that far. Oh, by the way, those two women..."

Schafter came a step closer and lowered his voice to a confidential whisper.

"... those two women with you, who were they?"

"The sisters of one of the baroness's maids," said Michiel. "They're from Uddel. You know, over by Elspeet. They had a wedding in Zwolle today and the baroness said they could use her carriage. So Aaltje asked if I'd take them."

"I see," said Schafter. "And didn't Aaltje have to go with them to the wedding?"

"Yes. She went as well."

"Then it's strange that I saw her this morning on this side of the IJssel."

Michiel blushed. "Th-then she must have been unexpectedly called back for some reason," he stuttered.

Schafter looked up at the sky. "Those sisters of Aaltje's.

They weren't by any chance a couple of men in disguise, were they?" he casually asked.

"Of course not. Where did you get that idea from?" said Michiel, trying to sound indignant.

"Oh, I was just wondering. One of them seemed to have a rather masculine face."

"I need to get going," said Michiel.

"Listen, Michiel," said Schafter, "you can trust me, you know. I know people say I'm on the wrong side, but it's not true. I need to get a couple of people across the river too. If you have any tips, then tell me. I swear to you I won't abuse your trust."

Shivers ran down Michiel's spine. The man was so brazen!

"I don't know what you're talking about. I don't know anything about any tips. It was two women from Uddel— and that's all. And I don't understand why it's any of your business either. Goodbye, Schafter."

Michiel strode off. He always made such a mess of everything. Absolutely everything. What was he going to do now?

That same afternoon, Van Dijk the ferryman was taken prisoner.

A stranger took his place. The baroness was placed under house arrest. Until her role in the clandestine crossings had been investigated, she was not allowed to leave her home. No one knew what punishment the German soldiers received. The baroness had outwitted so many of them over the months. The last squad leader lost his sergeant's stripes though—that news did get through to the villagers.

Once again, Michiel, who felt terribly guilty, expected that he would be taken in and questioned. They would surely want to know where he'd taken the two women. Once again, he approached the house cautiously when he returned home. Once again, he was so nervous that he could hardly eat and had to keep visiting the toilet every ten minutes. And once again, nothing happened. No one asked about him. No one was interested in him. Had Schafter not revealed his name? Did he feel sorry for Michiel and want to spare him? But it wasn't as if he'd been at all pleasant to Schafter. Michiel had no idea what was going on. More than ever, he wished that the Allies would hurry up and liberate them.

A fortnight later, the preliminary investigation was finished. The baroness's role had been established, and a sergeant, with two privates, went to arrest her.

They found the door locked and the shutters closed. The sergeant tugged on the bell repeatedly.

A window on the first floor opened and the baroness called down: "Clear off!"

"I order you to open this door. I am here to arrest you," said the sergeant solemnly.

"Away with you. No one arrests a Weddik Wansfeld."

The sergeant didn't quite know what to do. So he tried a different approach.

"Baroness, would you mind accompanying me to the command post? The commander of the garrison would like to speak to you."

"That's considerably better," said the baroness. "But the answer is no. If the commander wishes to speak to me, he will have to come here."

"Please, Baroness," the sergeant begged her.

The only answer was the window closing. All the sergeant could do was go back and make a report.

In the afternoon, an officer appeared, this time with five men and a battering ram. The events of the morning were repeated. Again the bell was rung, and again the baroness appeared at the upstairs window.

"If you do not open this door immediately, I will have my men ram it open," bellowed the officer, who was a large man.

"Do what you must," said the baroness.

The men lined up, brought the ram into position, and pounded it into the heavy, metal-studded front door. Then there was the sound of a shot and a scream from one of the soldiers. He'd been hit in the arm.

"Donnerwetter!" cursed the officer. He had glimpsed the baroness behind the balustrade of the balcony—and she had a gun. "This will cost you your life," he shouted up at her.

"It was a warning shot in an arm," the baroness called back. "The next time I'll aim for a head. Yours."

"The woman is insane," grumbled the officer. It seemed safer to seek the protection of the trees across the road. Was he really going to have to storm the house with his five men? Lives might be lost. Besides, the commander had told him to treat the baroness with courtesy. The commander, the son of an estate manager, had deep respect for the gentry. This was madness though. You couldn't sacrifice a few men just to arrest an old woman! Should he throw a couple of hand grenades through the windows? What would the commander think about that? He decided to go back and make a report as well. He had no better ideas and he was really rather tired of the whole business.

Nothing else happened that day, but the next morning at half-past ten the commander of the garrison came along in person. He politely rang the bell and—this was starting to become a habit—the baroness appeared at the upstairs window.

"Baroness," said the commander, "would you do me the favour of inviting me inside?"

"Certainly," the baroness replied. "If you remove your pistol."

"It would be my pleasure."

The commander took off his belt and holster. Soon he heard the sound of bolts sliding and the rattle of a chain. The door opened. He stepped inside to find that the baroness, impeccably dressed in a long morning gown, was aiming a large military pistol at him. She indicated that he should move along the corridor, and then slid the bolts on the door. She even put the heavy chain back on the hook.

"That's a nice pistol you have there," said the commander, more calmly than he felt. He didn't like the casual way the baroness was playing with the trigger.

"My husband was in the hussars," she explained. "I also have an army rifle and a double-barrelled shotgun. And sufficient ammunition."

"Do you know that the possession of weapons carries the death penalty?" asked the commander.

"I am aware of that. Please, sit down. Unfortunately I'm unable to offer you anything, as my staff are in the music room."

"In the music room?"

"Indeed. Along with the other residents. They're a bunch of cowards. So I sent them into the music room and locked the door."

She really has gone insane, thought the commander. There she sat, aiming the gun precisely at his heart. He had no doubt she would pull the trigger if he made the slightest attempt to disarm her.

"Madam, we are at war. I must ask you to accompany me."

"Where to?"

"The barracks."

"So that you can condemn me and execute me," said the baroness. "You just informed me that I could receive the death penalty for the possession of weapons. I have resisted arrest and shot one of your men in the arm. You also think I have something to do with the Koppel ferry. No, my dear commander, I have decided that I will not allow myself to be arrested, not even by the master race."

The commander, in spite of all his admiration for the aristocracy, was beginning to lose his temper.

"Give me the pistol, Baroness."

She responded by cocking the gun.

"I will have you removed from this house by force."

"So why didn't you do that yesterday?"

"That is my concern."

The baroness stood up. She considered the conversation to be over.

Furiously, the commander strode back down the hallway to the front door. *When she slides back the bolts, I'll knock the pistol from her hand*, he thought. But he didn't get the chance. The baroness indicated with a nod of her head that he should undo the bolts himself and remove the chain from the hook.

"You are making a big mistake, Baroness," he said by way of farewell.

"Compared to the actions of the German Reich, any other mistake is trivial," replied the baroness.

With those words, she closed the door behind him.

The next morning, a tank drove up to the white house on the IJssel. The commander of the garrison had spent all night pondering the problem and believed that he had found a solution that was worthy of a baroness, particularly this one.

"Baroness," he called, sticking the top half of his body out of the gun turret.

The baroness appeared at the upstairs window.

"Are you prepared to surrender?"

"Just a moment," she said.

Then a small door at the back of the house opened and all the residents filed out. All of them, except for the baroness. Her maids, her butler, her nieces, her brother-in-law, her son-in-law and, finally, her daughter.

"Mother, come with us," she pleaded.

"So that I can be shot dead by those criminals at six a.m. tomorrow in some barracks yard? No, thank you. I'm too old to be a prisoner. And too proud."

Sobbing, the daughter followed the others. The baroness carefully bolted the door. She went to the balcony, a gun in her hand.

"Commander!"

"I am listening, Baroness."

"Will you note that my family and staff have nothing to do with this affair? None of them has ever spoken a word to any of your men. I am responsible—and I alone."

"Noted," said the commander. "Now surrender, Baroness."

The baroness aimed the gun and fired a bullet, which narrowly missed his head. The commander ducked down into the tank and closed the hatch. The baroness calmly returned inside and headed to the dining room, which was lined with paintings of her ancestors.

"Fire," said the commander.

The tank began to fire. Twenty shells hit the white house. It was soon burning like a torch and the walls began to collapse.

When it was inconceivable that any living creature could possibly be found in the ruins, the commander finally gave the signal to retreat. As soon as the tank was gone, the baroness's family and all the locals who had been watching in horror came running and frantically tried to extinguish the fire.

After an hour's work, they dared to venture among the scorched and crumbling walls. They searched—and they found. The dowager Louise Adelheid Mathilde, Baroness Weddik Wansfeld, barely touched by the fire, lay beneath a pile of fallen bricks. She was wearing an orange sash. If the commander had taken the trouble to come and look, he would have seen from the defiant expression on her face that Germany was bound to lose the war.

The weeks went by. They became months. The shortest day, the 21st of December, came and went. Christmas 1944. A pitch-black Christmas. New Year's Eve. Would the new year bring peace? How many people asked themselves that question on that New Year's Eve? January, a long, cold month, with no fuel, barely any food. The famine in the big cities assumed alarming proportions. Many people had swollen stomachs as a result of severe malnutrition; some of them died. Those who had any strength left headed eastwards and northwards, to try to find food and bring it home for the little children and the elderly. The sad stream of food-seekers grew larger but moved more and more slowly. Everyone was exhausted.

The Germans were becoming more nervous, which also made them more cruel. The war was going badly on all fronts. They suffered losses on the eastern front, where the Russian armies were advancing. They had already had to surrender their positions in the south. In the west, the Allies had liberated France, Belgium and the southern Netherlands, and now they were pushing in an easterly direction, towards the *Heimat*, the homeland, Germany itself. Hitler was going to lose the war. No one in their right mind could doubt it now.

And then? Would the Allies treat the Germans' homeland the same way the Germans had treated the Netherlands, Belgium, France, Norway, Denmark, Czechoslovakia, the Balkans, North Africa, the Middle East, and Poland and Russia in particular? What would be in store for them when the concentration camps were discovered, the death camps where millions of innocent people had been eradicated as if they were vermin?

What remained of that proud country with its superior armies and its invincible *Führer*, Adolf Hitler? Oh yes, Hitler was certainly still talking about the ultimate, total triumph, about the secret weapon he had up his sleeve, about the invincibility of the Germanic race. But who still believed it? Bitterness filled the hearts of the German soldiers and, wherever they still held power, the shots of the execution squads rang out night and day.

Meanwhile, Erica had finally plucked up the courage to remove the plaster cast from Jack's leg. She would much rather have fetched the doctor who had treated Jack after his injury, but no matter how hard they thought, how Jack struggled to remember a name, they had no idea who it could have been. Dirk was the only one who knew and he was in prison in Amersfoort; his parents had received a brief notification.

Erica was afraid that the leg wasn't healing properly. When the plaster came off, they saw a large bump in the spot where the leg had broken. Maybe that wasn't unusual, but the leg also appeared to be slightly crooked. It still hurt when Jack tried to walk on it. Even so, he practised walking every day, and over time he began to improve—but he wouldn't be winning the 100-metre sprint any time soon, that much was clear.

The wound in his shoulder wasn't healing as it should either. Thanks to Erica's care, the infection had at least cleared up. She changed the bandage twice a week and kept the wound completely clean. But the wound wouldn't close.

"It's no wonder, given the state of this hospital," the trainee nurse grumbled. "Bed—a pile of dry leaves. Instruments—nail scissors and a kitchen knife."

"Properly sterilized, though," said Jack.

"Properly sterilized, yes," she agreed, "but not much to work with. Bread—stale. Vegetables—old. Potatoes—cold."

"But cooked with love," said Jack.

"That's true," said Erica with a smile, stroking his bearded cheek.

"And to drink—cold tea and buttermilk."

"I have to admit, I could do with a whisky," Jack revealed, who spoke Dutch almost perfectly now, although he still had a strong accent.

"Temperature—chilly and damp. Rehabilitation..."

"What did you say?"

"Rehabilitation. You need someone to help you walk again. And some space to practise. All you've got is two yards by two, minus the area taken up by the afore-mentioned pile of dry leaves, a rickety chair and a table. Doctor—none."

"Medical staff," said Jack. "Only the very finest."

"How am I ever going to get you well again in these conditions?"

"Oh," said Jack, "just remind yourself that when I'm back in good health, I'll have to do my utmost to get back to England. That's what the rules of our air force say. Would you like that? I know I'm a burden to you, of course, but still..."

"No, darling, of course not," said Erica, and that put an end to her complaints about his slow recovery.

In the meantime, Michiel was struggling with his guilt. The events surrounding the Koppel ferry and Baroness Weddik Wansfeld had shocked him deeply. He'd gone to her funeral, along with at least a thousand other people who'd had the same idea. It had been a demonstration of their admiration for the baroness, and a demonstration *against* the Germans too.

The commander of the garrison had sent a wreath, as he also wanted to show his respect for the woman. Everyone had thought that very sporting of him.

None of these people know that it was all my fault, Michiel had thought, as he stood there in the cemetery. Not the minister, who was brave enough to speak out against the Germans in his eulogy. Not the baroness's daughter, who scattered flowers on her mother's coffin. And not the unknown person who had sent a bouquet tied with an orange ribbon with "Long Live the Queen" written upon it.

The worst thing was that Michiel himself didn't know what he'd done wrong. He didn't know last time, with Bertus, and he didn't know this time either. What should he have done differently? If he had to take two Jewish men across to the other side of the IJssel again, would he be able to come up with a better way, a safer way? Everything he did went wrong. His actions had got all kinds of people into hot water, except for him. But he'd been so careful. Was he just a child, after all, too young for such responsibility? One of these days, they'd catch Jack as well, and that would be his fault too. That really would put the tin lid on it.

He decided that in future he'd get involved with illegal activities as little as possible. After all, he didn't seem to be very good at it. He visited Jack only once a week. Erica did the rest, and she did it surprisingly well. And he'd always thought he was so much better than his big sister! Ha, as if! He made a mess of everything. Should he leave Jack entirely to Erica? No, he couldn't quite bring himself to do that. He was the one who had received the letter from Dirk, so he was the one who was responsible for Jack. He doubled up on his precautions, worried himself half to death about the mistakes he might make and how to avoid them, and went on visiting him once a week.

Whenever he saw Schafter, he made a big show of looking the other way. The traitor must realize by now that Michiel was aware who had reported the baroness to the Germans. Michiel wanted him to know what he thought about that, even if Schafter hadn't given his name to the Germans. If he thought Michiel was grateful, then he was most mistaken.

Michiel had his cross to bear during the war, and it was not a light one.

As for little Jochem, he was constantly getting into scrapes. One day, when Erica and Michiel weren't at home and Mother was busy in the kitchen, he decided to climb onto the roof. He started by making his way to his brother Michiel's room up in the attic. That wasn't allowed, but Jochem wasn't in the mood for following rules.

When he got to Michiel's room, he forgot the reason for his visit for a moment, as his big brother had so many interesting things to pick up and look at. There was a collection of shells, for instance, and an old telephone and some cables and an atlas that was open at a map of France. Jochem touched just about everything, managed to crush two shells, picked up a pencil and drew a new border between France and Germany, as if he were General Eisenhower, the supreme commander of the Allied Forces, and then finally he had a telephone conversation with himself that ended with the declaration that he was about to climb out onto the roof. Then he opened the window.

Great. From the bed, it was easy enough to climb out and soon he was sitting in the gutter. The gutter, full of green slime and dry leaves, was a bit slippery. Oh well, slippery or not, it was too nice up there not to go for a little walk. He could look down onto the neighbours' roof—which would give him something to show off about to Joost, the boy next door. Feeling very pleased with himself, he made his way around the corner. That side of the house wasn't that interesting. He found himself looking at the blank wall of the town hall, which was no fun. He quickly reached the next corner. Good, now he was on the side facing the street—that was much better. He saw the baker looking up and stopping his cart. And look, there was Miss Van de Ende rushing out of her house with her hands in the air. And more people, all of them shouting.

What did they want? Was there something going on by the front door? He leant forward to look over the edge of the gutter. And finally he saw the dizzying drop yawning beneath him. If he fell, he'd be dead. Then he realized that the people were shouting up at him.

Suddenly Jochem felt afraid. He knelt down and clung to the edge of the gutter. His bottom lip started trembling and two minutes later he was wailing.

For once, Mrs Van Beusekom's mind had not been on Jochem. Her head was so full of worries about Erica and

Michiel. She could tell they were getting up to things she didn't know about. As always, her thoughts then turned to her husband, who was dead and wouldn't be able to help her bring up Jochem, who desperately needed his guidance. But where had Jochem got to? She walked to the front room, into the garden, looked in the shed, opened the cellar door.

"Jochem!"

No reply.

She'd already placed her foot on the bottom step to go upstairs and look, when the doorbell rang. She quickly took off her apron and opened the door.

"Mrs Van Beusekom, did you know your son's up on the roof?"

She dashed outside, where what must have been about twenty people had already gathered, and looked up. Her heart skipped a beat.

"Jochem, stay there. I'm coming!"

Would *she* have to rescue him from the roof? She couldn't even climb over the garden fence, and she felt dizzy when she stood on a chair.

"That gutter is completely rotten," said one of the men. "No work's been done on it since the war began, and it was already looking a bit shaky back in 1940. You could kick a hole in it just like that, I'm telling you."

"Mummy!" Jochem howled.

"Maybe we could reach him over the top of the roof, across the tiles," said another man. "Get a couple of men up on the ridge of the roof, and then lower someone down to the lad on a rope. But how would you get up there?"

"There's a window at the back," said Mrs Van Beusekom quickly. "Do you have a rope?"

"Yes, at home," said the man. "I'll go and fetch it."

"That'll take too long," someone suddenly said in German. "The boy can scarcely keep his balance. He's going to fall at any moment. May I go through your house?"

It was a German soldier who had spoken.

"Of course," Jochem's mother whispered, feeling rather bewildered.

The soldier leant his bicycle against the fence and ran into the house. He took the stairs two, three steps at a time and was soon wriggling out through the roof window. As he dropped down into the gutter, it bent beneath his feet.

"Rotten," the soldier muttered. "Old and rotten."

Leaning as close as he could to the tiles, he shuffled along the gutter, the same way Jochem had gone. When he reached the front of the house, the street below was packed with people. Mrs Van Beusekom had followed him at first, but then had returned to join the crowd, as she couldn't see Jochem through the roof window anyway.

When Jochem saw the man approaching, he stopped crying. Step by step, the soldier inched forward. Suddenly a cry of horror went through the crowd. The brave German's left boot had shot through the decaying gutter. He was only able to save himself by quickly falling forward and lying full-length in the gutter.

Jochem had been terrified when the stranger suddenly fell towards him, but now there was a strong hand around his left leg. It was such a good feeling.

"Now we will crawl along together," the German soldier said in broken Dutch.

Gently, he pushed Jochem ahead of him. They went around the other side of the house. The soldier's left knee was hanging above the drop and his foot was anchored in the gutter.

"Any minute now the whole thing's going to come tumbling down," muttered the man down below, who had already expressed his doubts about the condition of the gutter.

Mrs Van Beusekom stood with her hands clasped to her chest, barely able to breathe. "Save him, save him, save him," she prayed to herself.

After what seemed like an eternity, the two of them reached the back of the mayor's house. The soldier stood up carefully, leaning against the roof tiles, and pushed Jochem up to the window. Before long, the little lad was inside, in the arms of his mother, who had come running upstairs. The soldier was soon out of harm's way too. Mrs Van Beusekom took his hand.

"I-I don't know what to say," she stammered.

The man smiled, gave Jochem's cheek a friendly pinch and strode back downstairs.

"Wait, wait," cried Mrs Van Beusekom, but he was already outside and climbing onto his bike.

People respectfully stepped aside to let him through.

"Bravo," someone said, but the praise drifted away on the breeze.

The others were struck dumb. And then the soldier disappeared around the corner.

"A German?" Michiel asked in absolute amazement. "One of the Krauts?"

"Yes, a German soldier. One of Hitler's henchmen. An enemy of our people."

Mrs Van Beusekom was still pale, after all that she had been through. Jochem was as cheerful as ever, though. He'd already more or less forgotten what had happened.

Michiel went outside and looked up... He saw the broken gutter. He saw how high it was. Still shaking his head in surprise, he came back inside.

"Mother, why did a German have to save him? What was everyone else doing? Were they just standing around watching? And what about you?"

"There was no way I could save him. You know what a hero I am when it comes to heights. Everyone else was talking and trying to work out what to do. I don't think they felt brave enough to go up there either. It was terrifying. Did you see the place where his foot went through the gutter?"

"Was it really that dangerous?"

"Yes. It's a wonder he didn't fall to his death."

Erica had come home by now and she wanted to hear the story too. Her first reaction was to go and give Jochem a cuddle. She wasn't too surprised that it had been a German who had rescued him. But Michiel still couldn't quite get over it.

"But *why*, *why* did he do it?"

"Well, I suppose he must simply have been a nice man," said Erica.

"A German? A nice man? So what's he doing here?"

"Michiel," said Mrs Van Beusekom, "there are eighty million Germans. And whether you like it or not, some of them are good people, people who aren't happy about this war either. We don't like the Germans—you don't and I don't and Erica doesn't—but, whichever way you look at it, we shall have to be grateful to this one particular German. I'm certainly grateful to him, in any case."

"He could have been one of the firing squad," said Michiel stubbornly.

"I don't think so. And even if... No, I really don't think he could have been."

"You don't have to be part of a firing squad if you really don't want to," said Erica.

Michiel didn't reply. It was so much easier to hate *all* Germans. And he had to admit to himself that this soldier had behaved a great deal more nobly than all their neighbours put together. He looked at his brother's cheeky little face. A fall from that height onto the cobbles...

"Alright then, just this one," he growled. "The other seventy-nine million, nine hundred and ninety-nine thousand, nine hundred and ninety-nine are still murderers."

"I'm sure it's not quite as many as all that," said Mother. "But fine, if you've let one sheep over the ditch, others will surely follow. Come on, Jochem. It's bedtime."

"I'm never going out onto the roof again," said Jochem. "Only if that nice man comes with me."

II

It was a Wednesday afternoon and Michiel was getting ready to visit Jack. He popped a rucksack into his bike bag, with a couple of sandwiches, two apples, a bottle of milk, a small pan of cold, cooked brown beans and a piece of ham inside it.

Not a bad haul this time, he thought, as he cycled towards Dagdaler Wood. When he got there, he didn't immediately take the path to the young spruce plantation though, as someone was cycling behind him. Instead of going left, he went right. After a few hundred yards, he stopped and went back. The road was deserted now, so he headed into the woods. As usual, he hid his bike among the bushes and continued on foot. He reached the north-eastern section without running into anyone, and then dropped onto all fours and began the usual crawl. Jack heard him coming, even though Michiel was pretty stealthy by now, and the pilot was standing in the entrance to the cave, waiting for him.

"Don't be startled," he said. "But we have a visitor."

In spite of the warning, Michiel was still shocked. It couldn't be Erica. She'd been at home when he left.

"Who is it?"

"Take a look for yourself."

He went into the hideout and saw someone lying on the makeshift bed. As his eyes became used to the darkness, he realized who it was.

"Dirk!"

"Hello, Michiel."

Dirk sat up. He looked terrible! His nose was crooked. One of his eyes was so swollen that you couldn't even see it. There was a nasty graze on his left cheek. His mouth hung open—apparently he couldn't shut it properly.

"Dirk, what on earth have they done to you?"

Dirk tried to smile. But it was more of a grimace.

"Just as well I don't have a mirror."

"Did you escape?"

"Yes. Jumped off the train. The night before last. Hey, have you brought any food? I haven't eaten for two days. Hid in a hedge all day yesterday. Froze half to death. Walked here last night. Or rather, stumbled."

"More like tumbled," said Jack. "I almost shot him dead. He came crashing through the trees like a one-man platoon."

"Because I was almost unconscious," said Dirk.

Michiel opened up his rucksack and started handing the food to Dirk.

"Anything soft, please. Those beans, they'll do nicely. And milk. Lovely. I've hardly got any teeth left in my mouth. Sorry, Jack, I'm afraid you're going to miss out on most of the meal this time. Why don't you have the apples? I can't bite into them anyway."

"Don't worry about me," said Jack.

"I'll bring more," said Michiel. "Maybe today, but if not, tomorrow."

"Do you think you could bring another blanket?" asked Jack.

"I'll try."

Dirk ate everything he could manage to chew.

"I'm sorry, Jack. I seem to be taking over," he said when he'd finished. "I'm eating your food, I'm using your bed. I know I'm a nuisance."

"Well, it's your place really," said Jack.

"Michiel's taken good care of you, though?"

"He has."

"And he's even taught you Dutch."

"He did that by himself mostly, with the help of a book," said Michiel modestly. "But I'm sure he picked up a thing or two from Erica as well."

"Your sister?"

"Yes, sorry about that. She's practically moved in."

"I'm not sorry," said Jack.

"So, the leak—was that because of Erica?"

"Leak? What do you mean?"

"Well, someone gave us away."

"Not Erica. She didn't get involved until after the raid on the rations office, anyway."

"But somebody must have told the Germans about the raid. It was all just one big leaky sieve. Why do you think they came for Bertus, for instance? Jack told me about that. Did you let anyone read that letter, Michiel?"

"No. Of course not. I'm certain no one read it. I hid it in one of the chickens' nesting boxes. But what about you, Dirk, did you... I mean, they tortured you. Didn't you give them Bertus's name? I thought..."

Everyone was silent. Dirk had fallen back onto the bed again. He'd closed his eyes, and he looked exhausted.

"They beat me to within an inch of my life," he said quietly, "but I swear to you that I didn't give anything away."

He was breathing with difficulty through his damaged nose. Jack gestured to Michiel: *leave him be*.

"I'll see what food and blankets I can rustle up. Be back tomorrow afternoon at the latest," whispered Michiel. "Can you cope by yourselves until then?"

Jack nodded.

"Don't take any unnecessary risks. We'll manage."

"OK, see you then. Take good care of him."

"Roger."

Michiel set to work gathering as much food as he could. He went to see Mr Coenen, a farmer who was a good friend of his, and bought ham, eggs, butter and cheese. He begged a loaf of bread from the baker. The big box in the attic provided another couple of horse blankets. Buying the provisions cost him nearly all his money; that was going to be a problem in the days ahead.

Unfortunately, by then it was too late to go to the woods. He'd have to wait until the next day. When morning came, he was lucky. His mother said she was popping out with Jochem for an hour or so. That gave him a chance to boil the eggs. He even remembered to take some salt. The problem was: how could he get to the wood without being noticed, when he was carrying such a large package?

So Michiel decided to split the delivery. First he took one blanket, with some of the food wrapped up inside, which he hid close to the place where he usually began his crawl through the trees. Then he went home for the rest. As far as he could tell, no one had shown any more interest in him than usual, and by about eleven o'clock he was making his way through the young spruces, struggling to drag the two parcels behind him.

Dirk seemed to have perked up a little. There was more colour in his cheeks and his one eye looked bright, although the other was still swollen shut.

To Michiel's surprise, the pile of leaves had doubled in size.

"Where did all those leaves come from?" he asked suspiciously.

"Oh, they blew in here by themselves," said Jack.

"Really? There wasn't a breath of wind at home."

"Well, if you really want to know, I went out yesterday at dusk to that beech wood over there, and I fetched some leaves. I promise no one saw me, though."

"How did it go with your leg?"

"Fine."

"Well, that's good news. Congratulations."

"Thank you."

When Michiel had unpacked everything, the two young men were delighted and full of praise for him. Then there was silence, as they satisfied their hunger.

After everyone had finished eating, Michiel said, "I have a problem."

"Me too," said Dirk. "More like six. What's yours?"

"I've run out of money. The local farmers aren't profiteers, but I still have to pay them something for what they give me."

"I've got an idea," said Dirk after some pondering.

"That's good. Let's hear it."

"Talk to my mother. She needs to know I'm safe. Not my father, though. He'd be so scared that he'd end up giving everything away. Mother can tell him later, and then at least he won't know that you have anything to do with it. Just tell her that I'm in good shape, but I can't go to see her yet because it's not safe. And say that I'll need a food package every week, which you can deliver. She'll sort everything out, you'll see."

"Great. Then that's what I'll do."

Again, they sat in silence for a while, and then Dirk said, "What's the weather like?"

"Not bad. A bit cloudy."

"That's better than clear. We could do without frost, even with the blankets you brought. Reckon it's going to stay that way?"

"I don't know much about the weather. And, of course, we haven't had a radio for ages."

"I'll go and take a look at the sky myself."

Dirk walked to the entrance. He was limping so badly that Michiel couldn't help wincing.

"Did they do that to you?"

Dirk nodded.

"You know I've got a score to settle with the man who gave me away, don't you? I'll tell you something. I jumped off the train at Stroe. A good friend of mine lives not far from there, in Garderen, and I could have gone into hiding with him. But I came here instead. That's because I'm determined to find out who the traitor is around here."

"It's Schafter," said Michiel.

"Schafter? How do you know that? I thought Schafter was..."

"You thought Schafter was what?"

"I'm not sure. Maybe he really is a collaborator—who knows? I never would have thought it, though. I reckoned he was just pretending to be in cahoots with them for some reason. But I could be wrong."

"Yes. You're wrong," said Michiel. "I have the proof."

"Go on then. Out with it."

"It's a long story. You tell your story first, and then I'll tell you what I know."

"Alright," said Dirk, "here goes. I'll start at the beginning."

Dirk's Story

"At the beginning of the war, back in 1941, I was working in forestry. I was given the job of planting three plots of spruces, here, in Dagdaler Wood. I was about eighteen at the time, and although there wasn't much sign of the war around here yet, I decided on an impulse to make a hiding place. You never know when you might need one. No one would ever find it in the middle of a section of closely planted trees. I didn't tell anyone at all about it. Even later, when I joined the resistance, I still kept it to myself.

"The hiding place came in handy when I found Jack with a broken leg and a hole in his shoulder. First I took him to see a doctor who was in hiding nearby. The doctor was caught soon after that. I have no idea where he got the plaster from. I think he cobbled it together himself somehow, out of glue and chalk or something."

"Erica said she thought the plaster was a bit odd," said Michiel.

"Anyway, Jack got patched up and I dragged him to this hideout."

"As we already know," said Michiel.

"Yes, but I don't know exactly what you know, do I? I thought we were both going to tell the whole story, weren't we?"

"Sorry. Please go on," said Michiel.

"I didn't tell the other resistance members anything about Jack," continued Dirk. "I wasn't entirely sure that everyone was to be trusted. You know, one of the members was—and maybe still is—a certain Schafter. He sometimes said that he went along with the Germans just to pull the wool over their eyes. I always believed him. Going by what you've said, Michiel, I'm afraid I may have been too trusting. Anyway, I didn't say anything about Jack, and if you think about it, Jack's hiding place here is just about the only thing that hasn't been given away. That makes you think, doesn't it? So, last autumn, our commander gave us the order to raid the rations office in Lagezande. Three of us. Me, Willem Stomp, who's now dead, and another man who escaped, and I'd better not tell you his name. The commander thought three men were enough. He said no one else knew anything about it."

"The commander? You mean Mr Postma?"

Dirk stared at Michiel, startled. "How do you know that?"

"Lucky guess. Go on."

"Well, I thought, if anything goes wrong, Jack's going to starve to death. If I gave my letter directly to Bertus, who was also in the resistance, then he'd know I had something to hide. I didn't want to risk that. So I gave it to you, Michiel. If everything had gone according to plan, Bertus would never have found out about the letter's existence. He still doesn't know anything about it, as far as I'm aware. I'd always thought you seemed pretty level-headed, and so I decided I could trust you."

"Well, even though I messed up just about everything, you were right to trust me," Michiel said sadly.

"Yes, I believe you, Michiel. But listen. At the rations office in Lagezande, we walked right into an ambush. They were waiting for us. Do you understand what that means? Someone had betrayed us. But who? Who knew about the plans? The three of us who were going to carry it out. Mr Postma, who said he'd told no one else. And you, Michiel. That was it."

"Could the third man, the one who got away, have just pretended to escape and actually given away the plan beforehand?"

"I thought about that too. It seems very unlikely to me. I'll tell you why in a minute."

"What happened during the raid?"

"That's the thing. We'd agreed that the third man would be on the lookout and that Willem and I would go inside. The Germans had probably expected the third man to stand guard close to the door, because they'd hidden behind the hedge just by the rations office. But we'd agreed that he'd walk in a big circle around the building to make sure no one came near. So he'd already stayed behind to take up position when Willem and I reached the office. We'd just opened the front door when the Germans leapt out. With at least fifteen guns aimed right at us. I knew we didn't stand a chance, so I put my hands in the air. But Willem ran into the office, vaulted over the counter, and then bolted through the door into a back room, where he tried to escape through the window. He'd underestimated the Krauts though. They'd also positioned a couple of men around the back of the building and they shot him dead on the spot. I heard the shots but I didn't know exactly what had happened. By then they were pushing me towards their truck. 'Where is the third man?' they kept snarling. Well, I played dumb, said I didn't understand any German—which is more or less true—and I told them it had just been the two of us. 'We already have the second one,' they grinned and they threw Willem's body into the truck. I tried to see if there was anything I could do to help him, but they hit me in the face and told me he was past help. And then they started going on about the third man again. What I want to know is: how were they so sure that there were three of us?"

Michiel and Jack had no answer for him.

"Someone gave us away, I'm sure of that. They knew exactly what we were planning. Maybe it was Schafter. Maybe he eavesdropped on our conversation with Postma. Maybe he found some of Postma's notes. I'm curious to hear what you have to say about it, Michiel. I just want to know. I want certainty. Because what I had to go through in prison, it was so... so...." He paused. "Whoever it was who sent me into that trap... I'm going to make sure he's punished."

Dirk gave a loud sniff before continuing his story.

"They went on looking for a long time, but they eventually gave up. And if it was the third man who betrayed us, would they really have kept looking for him that long? They took me to the barracks. Let me stew for three days. And then the interrogation began."

"Wait a moment," said Michiel. "You mean they didn't ask you straightaway about Bertus and the resistance and so on?"

"No, not until three days later."

"Then why did they come for Bertus the next day? To be honest, I was convinced that they'd tortured you so badly that you'd given them his name. Sorry about that, but then you did think I'd let someone read the letter too."

"Don't worry about it. So yes, they only started asking questions after three days. At first it was all fairly civilized. The commander isn't such a bad chap. He clearly wanted to find out if there was some kind of underground organization behind the raid. I denied it. I said that Willem and I had come up with the plan and carried it out by ourselves. He didn't really swallow that, but I don't think he knew for certain that I was lying. Then he started asking me about the third man. I told him yet again that there'd been no third man, but that time it was obvious that he knew it wasn't true. He told me I'd be wise to tell him who it was, because otherwise he'd hand me over to the SS. He said they had some good ways to make people talk. He wasn't wrong. I was transferred to Amersfoort. Again, they left me alone for a while at first. Then the SS interrogations began. They always made me strip naked, so that it hurt more when they kicked me with their big boots. 'The name! The name!' they kept yelling and I told them over and over again that there'd been only two of us, and then they'd knock me to the ground and two or three of them would kick me, aiming for my stomach and my face, until I was unconscious."

"And you still didn't give him away?" asked Michiel, pale with misery as he listened to Dirk's tale. "Why not? How could you bear it?"

"I don't know the answer to that myself," said Dirk. "Every time I lay there, back on my bunk, bruised and curled up in pain, I thought: *I can't keep doing this, next time I'll tell them everything I know.* But when I saw their vicious faces again, I didn't tell them after all.

"Then, one day, they didn't beat me up. The SS officer who always interrogated me was all smiles instead. He said that, for my own sake, I should reconsider and give them the name of the third man. All he'd get was a year or two in prison. He was being so pleasant that I almost fell for it. But then I remembered all the things they'd done to me, and I kept my mouth firmly shut. And that spiteful look came over his face again. I thought the beating was about to begin, but no, he told me to get dressed. I was only too happy to do so. But when I reached my socks, he told me to wait a moment. And said I should put my right foot on his desk. So I did. He took out a truncheon, gave it a stroke and then asked in a silky voice if I was sure there hadn't been a third man. 'Yes,' I said, 'absolutely certain.' So then he broke every one of my toes with his truncheon and invited me to put my other foot on the desk."

Michiel gasped. "The bastard," he said.

Jack just winced.

"Anyway," said Dirk, "my shoes were on the small side, but I still had to put them on; my toes are completely deformed now. The strange thing is that I didn't even mind it that much, because they left me alone for a long time after that. Let me tell you, I'd rather have broken toes than an interrogation every other day.

"Then, a few days ago, they decided to move us. No one told us where we were going. They put us on one of those trains with separate compartments, each with its own door, you know the kind. There were nine of us in each compartment, with one armed SS guard. I was determined to try to escape if the slightest opportunity presented itself. Most of the other eight lads looked like they'd been interrogated a few times too. If that was true, I was sure they'd dare to risk an escape attempt as well.

"When the train started moving, I soon noticed we were heading towards Apeldoorn. I knew the train always slows down between Amersfoort and Apeldoorn as it goes around the bend by Stroe. In a whisper, I suggested to the others that we should jump out of the train at that point. We weren't supposed to be talking, and I was counting on the SS man not knowing any Dutch. I was right about that, but his ears were working just fine; he whacked me in the ribs with the butt of his gun. The others had already got the message, though. But as we approached Stroe, we realized to our horror that the door was locked."

"So you tried to open the door with the guard there?" asked Michiel.

"By then, the guard was already... No, don't ask. Two lads from Rotterdam, who were sitting next to him, had taken care of that. But, anyway, the door was locked and that gave us a real fright. No need to wonder what would have happened if they'd found us in there with a dead Kraut, when we got to Apeldoorn. But yes, when your back's up against the wall, there's no telling what you can do—one of the boys used the soldier's bayonet to force the door open before we reached the bend. As the train slowed down, we jumped out, one after the other, all nine of us. One man didn't make it. He hit his head on a post."

"And the Germans didn't notice?"

"They certainly did. They shot at us through the windows. But it was pretty dark and luckily the train didn't stop. They didn't hit anyone. That was where our luck ended, though. The eight of us were discussing what we should do, stick together or go our separate ways, when a German patrol came along. Random bad luck. Of course we knew there were patrols by the railway lines, but the likelihood of them coming along right at that moment... Anyway, we heard them coming and we dived into a ditch. But they'd obviously heard something too, because one of them yelled out: 'Halt. Password.' He'd hardly spoken the words when Krijn, one of our gang, began shooting like mad. He was a commando or a paratrooper or something like that, and he'd been clever enough to take the Kraut's submachine gun from the train. He got at least three of them with that first round of shots. The others took cover and began shooting back. Except for Krijn, all we could do was try to make ourselves invisible—we had no weapons. 'Run!' Krijn yelled. 'I'll keep them busy.' So we all crept away, along the ditch, and looked for hiding places, every man for himself. The shooting went on for a while. I don't know whether Krijn got out of there alive, but it wouldn't surprise me. He didn't seem like the kind of man who'd be easy to kill. A real daredevil type. And I've already told you the rest. I hid in a hedge for a day, and I dragged my way here that night."

Telling the story had tired Dirk out. He fell back onto the leaves, with his hands behind his head.

"And now you can hardly walk?" asked Michiel.

"I can still manage a bit, or I'd never have got here from Stroe. When the war's over, maybe some surgeon will be able to put my toes right. My eyes and my nose and the other injuries should heal by themselves. Most of the damage to my face is because of the jump from the train, by the way. I landed badly. But that's enough about that. It's in the past, doesn't really matter. What I want to know is: who is the traitor here in De Vlank?"

"My money's still on Schafter," said Michiel.

"Really? Then tell me why Schafter hasn't shut down the entire underground group here. He knows everyone!"

Michiel had no reply.

"Shall I tell my story now?" he asked.

Dirk had closed his eyes.

"Maybe tomorrow, eh?" said Jack.

12

Michiel couldn't stop thinking about Dirk's story. It was on his mind for the rest of that day. His mother could tell that he was worrying about something, but she didn't ask any questions.

So, such things, such terrible things, really did happen. He kept remembering what his father had once said: "There are horrors in every war. Don't go thinking it's only the Germans. The Dutch, the British, the French—every nation has brutally murdered and tortured in times of war, in ways that would seem unimaginable in peacetime. So don't be fooled, Michiel, by the romance of war, heroism, sacrifice, excitement, adventure. War means injuries, grief, torture, imprisonment, hunger, hardship, injustice. There's nothing romantic about it."

Michiel knew for sure that he wouldn't have been able to bear the treatment that Dirk had received. He was full of admiration for him. It was such a relief that now at least he'd escaped his torturers' clutches. His mother needed to hear the news as soon as possible.

Michiel kept a close eye on the neighbours' house. Late that afternoon, he saw Mr Knopper going out, and he quickly hopped over the fence. He found Dirk's mother by the back door, taking out a pan of peelings.

"I've got a message for you," he said. "Can I come inside?"

"A message? Is it from Dirk?"

Michiel nodded. They walked together to the kitchen.

"Is it bad news? And how did you come to hear it?"

"No, no, it's good news," said Michiel. "Very good news, in fact. But you have to promise not to say anything about it to anyone, and not to ask me any questions."

"Yes, of course," said Mrs Knopper.

"Dirk's escaped. He's safe—for the moment, at least."

Mrs Knopper immediately forgot her promise.

"So where is he? How do you know? Is he alright? Can I see him? How did he escape? Why hasn't he come home?"

"It's too dangerous," said Michiel. "He's in fairly good health, that's all I can tell you. And he needs food. He's asked if you could put together a food parcel for him every week. I'll make sure he gets it."

"Of course I will. Gladly. I can tell my husband, though, can't I?"

"You can tell him Dirk's safe, but not that it was me who told you. Other than him, absolutely no one can hear about this."

"My lips are sealed. Just tell me if he's here, in De Vlank."

"He's... he's safe. That's all I can say," replied Michiel. "Bye, Mrs Knopper. And remember—don't tell your husband you heard it from me."

"No, I won't. I'll have a parcel ready tomorrow. Can't you tell me just a little bit more, Michiel? Can I go and visit him?"

"No, that's not possible, I'm sorry. But it's safer this way," said Michiel. "And now I really do have to dash."

"Bye, Michiel. Thanks, lad. I can't tell you how happy I am."

Michiel left with a light heart. He was sure Dirk's mother would prepare so much food that the problem of feeding Jack would be solved as well.

The next day it was Erica's turn to go to the hideout. Michiel decided to tell her everything. After all, it would be impossible to keep Dirk's return a secret from her. So they went there together the next day. Michiel went first, with the package from Dirk's mother, and Erica followed about ten minutes later.

Dirk felt a little better than the day before. He insisted that Michiel should tell him his story now. Which Michiel did, in detail. He described exactly what he had done with Dirk's letter from minute to minute, and he explained how everything had gone against him that day when he'd wanted to visit Bertus and, in particular, how Schafter had cycled along with him, and how, finally, the next day, he'd talked to Jannechien and found out that, again, it was Schafter who had shown the Germans where to go.

Dirk was not convinced. It could all just have been a coincidence, he said. But when Michiel told him about the

159

Koppel ferry, about the arrest of Van Dijk the ferryman and the death of the baroness, and especially his conversation with Schafter shortly before, he agreed that it did all sound very suspicious.

"How are we going to prove it?" Michiel wondered.

"Tricky," said Dirk. "Very tricky. In any case, Michiel, I'd like to ask you to go to see the commander"—he didn't refer to Postma by name because of Erica, who didn't need to know exactly who the commander was—"and to warn him to be careful around Schafter. Tell him it's a message from White Leghorn, and that you received it from a friend."

"Yes. From Uncle Ben or someone," said Michiel. "He's in the underground too. White Leghorn, is that your code name in the resistance?"

Dirk nodded.

They talked for a while about this and that. The conversation naturally came back around to the death of Michiel and Erica's father.

"Why was it that they took the prisoners?" Dirk wanted to know.

"A dead German was found in the woods not far from here," Michiel told him. "With his head bashed in. The Germans wanted to know who'd done it. So they arrested ten men and announced that if the culprit didn't give himself up within twenty-four hours they'd hang those ten men from the chestnut trees on the village green. And, of course, the killer didn't hand himself in—that's the kind of coward he was. So they shot five men dead, including Father. They didn't hang them, though—that would have been even worse. Hey, what's wrong?"

Dirk and Jack had turned deathly pale and were staring at Michiel and Erica with grim expressions.

"What's wrong? You already knew that Father was dead," said Erica.

Neither of them said anything. Erica looked at one, then the other. Suddenly Dirk dropped to the ground, with his head on his arms, sobbing like a child. His whole body shook. Jack slumped in a corner, hiding his head in his hands.

"Why are you so upset?" Michiel asked helplessly.

But a terrible suspicion was dawning on Erica. She walked over to Jack and started shaking him by the shoulder.

"Did the two of you?..."

She pulled his hands away from his face. He looked at her desperately.

"Was it you two? Did you kill that German?"

"Yes," Jack whispered.

Erica let go of him. She walked out of the hideout as if in a trance. Even then, Michiel remembered the need for caution. He went after her and pulled her to the ground.

"Get down. You're sticking up above the trees."

Erica dropped to her knees and crawled through the saplings. Michiel followed her. They climbed onto their bikes and rode back to the village in silence.

"Let's not go home," Michiel said when they reached the high street. "We have to talk."

They cycled past their house and, with no need for discussion, headed straight for the Wigwam. It was a disused tumbledown barn where Erica and Michiel used to have a secret den, back when they were little and still played together. They'd made up hundreds of adventures at the Wigwam and had some real ones too. Sometimes they didn't go there for a while because Erica was off having fun with her friends or Michiel wasn't in the mood for "girls' stuff". But there always came a time when they wanted to play together, just the two of them. Then they'd go to the Wigwam.

When was the last time they'd been there? It must have been years ago. They leant their bikes against the barbed wire of the neighbouring field and went inside. Everything was just as before, except the barn was even more dilapidated now.

Erica sat down on an upturned rusty bucket, while Michiel paced back and forth.

"I'll never be able to forgive them," said Erica.

"It's an awful business," Michiel agreed. "They should have known, or at least Dirk should have known, that something like that would happen if the German was found. But you can't call Dirk a coward. What about everything he went through without giving up the third man's name?"

"That doesn't mean he'd have handed himself in if he hadn't been in prison when the Germans found that body.

He should have turned himself in immediately after doing it. Or at least Jack could have given himself up. He's in the army. They wouldn't have shot him for killing a German soldier. One soldier killing another, that's allowed."

"Yes," said Michiel, "but maybe they didn't think it all through properly."

"I don't understand," snapped Erica. "Two months ago, you said that if you ever got your hands on the man who did it, you'd beat him to a pulp. And now you're defending the two of them."

"So what do you suggest? Do you want to hand them over to the Krauts?"

"Have you gone mad?!"

"They're completely dependent on us. If we don't look after them, you might as well just hand them over to the Krauts."

Erica became lost in thought.

"Look, I'm as shocked as you are," said Michiel. "I loved Dad just as much as you did. But yesterday I also heard from Dirk's own mouth what he had to go through. Half an hour ago, I thought he was the toughest guy in the world. He did a stupid thing, but that doesn't make him weak or cowardly. I've done some pretty stupid things myself. One way or another, I'm to blame for Bertus being captured and for the baroness being killed."

"There's nothing you could have done about that."

"Did you see how devastated Dirk was? He was really crying."

"That's because he's in such a weak condition," said Erica. "He's completely broken. He's got no resistance left."

"Weak or not, you could see how terrible he feels about it."

"More like how guilty he is."

They sat in silence again for a while.

"And of course they'll be feeling terribly anxious, now that we've gone and left them," said Erica.

"I'm not too concerned about that," said Michiel. Now it was his turn to be harsh. "When Father was taken prisoner, we were anxious too."

"Yes, that was bad," whispered Erica. "It was awful. And it's not something you'd wish on anyone else."

Michiel looked at her. His sister's good nature always won out.

"We should at least give them the chance to tell us exactly what happened," he said.

"Do you think so?"

"Yes, I do."

"Right."

"Shall we go back there then?"

"What? Now?"

"Or leave them worrying for another night?"

"No, we can't do that," replied Erica.

With a weak smile, she stood up. She took hold of her brother's hand. "You're supposed to be the leader of our resistance group, aren't you? Then I'll follow your lead."

So they got on their bikes and rode back to Dagdaler Wood.

*

Dirk had calmed down in the meantime. He sat there, staring ahead with a gloomy expression on his face, but he'd managed to pull himself together. Jack's blank expression revealed very little.

"We're listening," said Michiel.

"I'll tell you my part first," said Jack. "Here goes. You know that I'm a pilot. I flew a Spitfire. My squadron was stationed at a temporary airstrip in the south, near Eindhoven. That day I was ordered to fly out over the IJssel and to shoot up any motorized vehicles I saw. It all went smoothly at first. Near Hattum I saw a German car. When they spotted me, the men leapt out and disappeared into the bushes. Shooting up the car was a piece of cake after that. It didn't use up much ammo, so I had enough to keep going. But the trouble began above Zwolle. They started firing anti-aircraft guns at me, and the flak was soon whistling around my ears. I tried to get out of there, but they hit my tail. I still had quite a bit of height though, and I wanted to try to escape the occupied zone, even though my rudder was playing up. So I flew directly south. Unfortunately, I'd just got out of range of the anti-aircraft guns when my engine went up in flames. Seems they'd hit the fuel tank too, and the leak had caused a fire. I had to bail out—and fast. I could see trees beneath me. That's no fun for a parachutist, but what else could I do? I had no choice. Luckily, my chute opened cleanly. *Well, Jackie,*

I thought to myself as I floated down. *Looks like it's life as a prisoner of war for you.* But then I realized that I couldn't see a single clearing below, just treetops, and that thought changed into a little white cross in a graveyard in a Dutch village. Anyway, I landed in a big oak. My foot got jammed in the fork of two branches, but the rest of my body kept going and, *crack,* my leg snapped like a matchstick. There I hung, dangling from my broken leg. It felt as if the world had turned upside down. It was pretty grim. Then, to my horror, down below, at the foot of the oak tree, I spotted a German soldier. There was a pistol in his hand and he was aiming it at me. 'Don't shoot,' I yelled, in English, because I didn't know how to say it in Dutch back then, of course. Oh, but that wouldn't have helped, would it? It should have been German. But the swine shot anyway. I felt it hit my shoulder and then I fainted, I think. I was sure I was a goner, I remember that much. And that's all I can tell you. I wasn't around for what happened next."

Michiel and Erica turned to look at Dirk, who cleared his throat.

"Right," he said, "this is where I come in. I was in the woods that day, making a note of the trees that needed thinning. I had my billhook with me. My ears pricked up when I heard some unusual noises nearby. At first I thought it was a deer and I wanted to see if I could hit it with my billhook. I'd been practising throwing it, just for a bit of fun at first, but later I got more serious about it. We could certainly put a bit of venison to good use, eh?

"Anyway, I stalked towards the noise as quietly as I could. I soon discovered it was a German soldier cuddling with some girl I didn't know, but then something really unexpected happened. Up above, I heard the sound of breaking branches and a shriek that startled the life out of all three of us: the German, the girl and me. It must have been you screaming, Jack, when your leg broke. But I have to say, those first few seconds, it sounded like the devil himself was descending on us.

"The girl leapt to her feet and ran away, wailing. That was the last I saw of her. The soldier had jumped up too. I saw him take out a pistol. He must have thought he was under attack, I imagine. Then I heard a shout in English— that'll have been you yelling 'Don't shoot'—and I realized that the peculiar, upside-down figure half-hidden by a parachute must be an Allied pilot who'd bailed out of a plane. The German had taken a shot by then and, well, I just saw red. I suppose the man acted out of fear and confusion, but maybe he was just a bloodthirsty killer. It's not uncommon among our Germanic friends. In any case, when he took aim for the second time, I swung my billhook and hurled it at him. It was the best throw of my life. Hit him right on the back of the head. If he'd been wearing his helmet, he'd have been fine, but he'd taken it off to kiss and cuddle. The thing was still lying there in the grass. And he was stone dead.

"I knew what a terrible situation I was in. I had a badly wounded British pilot, who was hanging upside down in a tree, unconscious, and I had to try to keep him out of enemy hands. And then there was the body of the German soldier I'd killed, and if that was found I'd end up against the wall, no questions asked. Same would go for hiding the pilot. I climbed up into the tree. I cut a length of cord from the parachute and tied it to Jack, then wrapped it around a branch a few times so I could slowly lower him to the ground. It was a hell of a job getting his jammed foot free, firstly because I could barely reach it and secondly because it meant I had to tug his broken leg this way and that. Luckily, Jack was still unconscious.

"To cut a long and gruesome story short, I eventually got him down. I took off my shirt and used it as a make-shift bandage for his wounded shoulder. He came round just as I was finishing. Unfortunately we couldn't really say anything to each other, though, because I don't know much English. But he knew I was worried about that dead German."

"I didn't understand much of what was going on," said Jack. "The pain in my leg was killing me."

"But you mimed burying something," said Dirk. "I knew full well that if they found a murdered Kraut, the whole village would be in serious danger. I considered all sorts of options, including handing myself in, I swear to you. But it's not that easy to walk straight towards your own death. Finally, I thought I'd come up with a good solution. *Hey*, I thought, *if a British pilot killed a German, that's just a simple act of war, isn't it? There's nothing the villagers could do about that.* But unfortunately I couldn't explain that to Jack. So I came up with the idea of wrapping the body in the parachute. The Germans couldn't have missed a British plane going down in the woods. If they found a dead German wrapped in a British parachute, wouldn't they come to the conclusion that their man had come off worst in a fight with the pilot? So, as best I could, I dug a hole with my billhook, but I couldn't dig very deep because of all the roots. I put the parachute around the German and covered him with a layer of soil. All I took was his pistol. It's the one that's on Jack's belt."

"I didn't hear anything about a parachute being found with the body," said Michiel.

"Maybe someone found it earlier and took the parachute," suggested Erica. "You know parachute silk is in real demand."

"Maybe," said Michiel.

"And I've already told you that I took Jack to a doctor who was in hiding nearby, and then about the struggle I had to bring him here," Dirk said, finishing his story. "A few weeks later I was captured myself. So now you know everything. So do I. And I know now that I should have handed myself in."

Something had come between them—between Michiel and Dirk, and between Erica and Jack. It was no longer a question of guilt, not after what Dirk had said. No one—not if they were being reasonable at least—could have said that either Jack or Dirk had done anything wrong. Certainly not Jack. He'd been in too much of a state to know much about anything. And as for Dirk... Michiel thought Dirk actually deserved a medal for his bravery. And yet now his father's death stood between them. *Everything that seems beautiful and noble and heroic about war,* Michiel thought bitterly, *gets spoilt, one way or another. Father was right: there's nothing romantic about war.*

After hearing Jack and Dirk's stories, Michiel and Erica apologized for running away and agreed that the whole disaster wasn't their fault, that Dirk had done the right thing and that, if anyone was guilty, it was whoever had stolen the parachute. No, not guilty, more like irresponsible, unthinking—although he should at least have come forward when the hostages were taken and informed the Germans that there'd been a parachute wrapped around the body. They told Dirk to stop feeling guilty. They even made jokes about Jack spying on courting couples from the air. But still...

It's going to take time, thought Erica. *But I'll get used to the idea. Jack's still the same man, after all. He hasn't done anything wrong. So that's alright then!*

And the brother and sister went on supplying their two older friends with food.

"But you know something? Keeping rabbits is a whole lot easier," said Michiel.

13

Even in times of darkness, famine and danger, the clock still goes on ticking. January went by. February went by. The stream of starving people from the west became wider and moved more slowly. They were weak and thin. The strongest ones, the young men, had either been dragged off to Germany, or had gone into hiding. No new mayor was appointed. Mrs Van Beusekom went on living with her children in the mayor's house, which every night was filled with hollow-eyed, stumbling, exhausted souls. Michiel went on thinking about the betrayal. He'd been through it all a thousand times. A thousand times, he came back to Schafter. And a thousand times, he still wasn't certain.

One Sunday afternoon, he went out for a walk with Uncle Ben. They strolled through the fields, where the winter rye was growing nice and green. They ambled past the meadows, where the young cows, the yearlings, didn't seem troubled by the gusts of March wind.

"The buds are swelling," said Uncle Ben, snapping a twig from an elder bush. "Spring is on its way. It's about time. The people in the big cities have suffered such bitterly cold weather this winter. There's no coal left. Masses of trees in the parks have been felled. The wooden sheds have been torn down. People did whatever they could to get a fire going, so they could warm their chilled bones and cook their tulip-bulb soup."

"Tulip-bulb soup?"

"Oh yes, tulip bulbs have become quite the delicacy. Remember the story of the siege of Leiden, back in the 1500s? People ate dogs and cats and rats. They came pretty close to eating their mayor. It's not yet come to that, but it's not far off."

"You're not wrong," said Michiel. He was only too well aware that people were hungry. Few had been as involved as him with the starving masses passing through the village.

"When do you think the war will be over?" he asked.

Uncle Ben shrugged. "I know a fortune-teller who's predicted the definite date of Hitler's surrender four times already. But the facts always prove her predictions wrong."

"Everyone says it can't go on much longer. They say the Allies are heading straight for Berlin, and so are the Russians."

"Don't start rejoicing too soon," said Uncle Ben. "Have you heard about what happened in the Ardennes?"

"In the Ardennes? No, what?"

"On 16th December the German troops, supported by a Panzer division under General Von Manteuffel, launched a powerful offensive in Belgium, in the Ardennes. The Allies were taken by complete surprise. They had no idea the Krauts were still that strong. Luckily, it failed, because the Germans couldn't take Bastogne. Who knows what would have happened otherwise? And don't forget their big weapons, the V1s and V2s. There are more and more of those terrible rockets raining down on London. People say they're developing other secret weapons too, but who knows for sure?"

"Don't the Americans have any secret weapons?"

"No idea. Let's hope so."

For a while, they were silent.

So Uncle Ben thinks the war could go on for a long time, thought Michiel. *A long time for Schafter and his pals to get up to their nasty tricks.*

"I wish," he said, thinking aloud, "that I knew a way to find out if someone is a traitor."

"A traitor? Who?"

"Someone here in the village."

"So who did he betray?"

"Oh, that's beside the point," said Michiel.

"I once had to deal with something like that," Uncle Ben told him.

"Really? What happened?"

"The man was in the same resistance group as me, but I didn't trust him. So, accidentally on purpose, I left a note lying around where I knew he'd find it. The note said where a Jewish family were hiding. And—surprise, surprise!—the next day there was a raid on that house."

"What happened to the Jewish family?" asked Michiel.

"There was no Jewish family, of course. I'd chosen a house where I knew the residents were pro-German. But I had my answer."

"So what did you do?"

Now it was Uncle Ben's turn to smile and say, "That's beside the point."

The idea appealed to Michiel. He must be able to do something similar with Schafter. But how was he going to get a note to him? He could just post it in his letter box. If he hung around until Schafter left the house, he'd be able to do it without being noticed. Schafter lived alone, so that wasn't a problem.

What should the note say, though? *Dear Mr Schafter, I wish to inform you that Mrs X has Jews in her house. Yours sincerely, Michiel van Beusekom.* No, of course not.

What, then?

To start with, there was no need for him to sign it. An anonymous letter. If Schafter ignored it, then there was no harm done. But whose house could he get the Nazis to raid? He didn't know for certain that anyone in the village was pro-German, except for Schafter himself.

"How do you know for definite if someone's collaborating with the Germans?" he said.

"Hmm," said Uncle Ben, "that's a tricky one. Didn't you say there's a man called Schafter in the village who's been acting suspiciously?"

"That's right," said Michiel, "but I don't know for sure." He wanted to keep his cards close to his chest. "Imagine if he really *was* sheltering Jews in his house. I'd never forgive myself."

"Hmm," said Uncle Ben again.

He thought for a moment.

"It doesn't have to be Jews, of course," he said then. "You could come up with something else. Like, say, that there are weapons hidden in that Green Cross building by your house. That's empty, isn't it? Let them raid that building."

Michiel had never thought his uncle was a fool, but now he was starting to believe he was a genius.

"Excellent," he said. "I'll send the man I suspect an anonymous letter and we'll see what happens."

Uncle Ben gave him a sidelong glance.

"Hey, my young friend," he said, "I don't want to stick my nose into your business, but aren't you perhaps getting too involved in things that you're too young for?"

"I'm not a child," said Michiel indignantly. "I'm sixteen."

"Well, blow me down," said Uncle Ben. "What an old man! Hey, look, you're already going grey at the temples. Or is it just fluffy little baby hairs?"

That was good enough reason for Michiel to give a nearby tree trunk a hard kick and, as a result, his uncle, who was walking underneath it, got a shower of drips and drops on his head.

When Michiel got home, he went straight to work. After a few failed attempts, he got the following message down on paper, disguising his handwriting:

The occupier needs to know that there are weapons hidden
in the Green Cross building.   E

The E was to make it more believable. It didn't really
mean anything. He wanted Uncle Ben to read the note,
but, as usual, his uncle had somewhere else to be. It was
probably for the best. The less other people knew about
you, the safer you were.

The next morning, he made his way to Schafter's house.
He was planning to hide behind some bushes about a
hundred yards from the house and wait. But he was in
luck. As he passed the grocer's, he saw Schafter inside the
shop. Good. Now he needed to walk on quickly, before
the man finished his shopping. At Schafter's house, he
stopped and looked around. He didn't see anyone he knew,
just the usual crowds filling the road. He dashed through
the gate and slipped the note into the letter box. Even if
a neighbour had spotted him, it wouldn't be a problem.
No one spoke to Schafter. Everyone avoided him as if he
had some kind of infectious disease.

After that, it was a case of waiting to see what happened. For the first twenty-four hours, Michiel could
hardly take his eyes off the Green Cross building. When
he was at home, he kept wandering over to the window
to see if anything was happening. But no. The building
was as lonely and abandoned as ever, and it stayed that
way all week. Not one German bothered even to glance
at it.

I'm still none the wiser, thought Michiel. *Either Schafter isn't a traitor, or he saw through the ruse and he's not falling for it.*

Uncle Ben came by another day and asked how Michiel's plan had gone.

"A complete failure," said the young would-be trapper, and left it at that.

Another week passed, in which nothing much happened, just the usual misery of the starving people passing through and a failed bombing of the barracks (the bombs all landed in a field). And then, fifteen days after Michiel had put the note in Schafter's letter box, that all changed. They came one afternoon. A truck stopped in front of the building, and five soldiers got out. They kicked open the door and went inside. Michiel saw it all from the living room.

"What are you looking at?" his mother asked.

"A raid on the Green Cross building."

Mrs Van Beusekom came to look.

"What on earth are they doing there? That place has been empty for three years."

"No idea," said Michiel, but he looked so triumphant that his mother was a little startled.

The soldiers stayed for half an hour. Then they got back into the truck and drove off, leaving the door ajar.

I'll go and see Dirk tomorrow, thought Michiel. He hadn't told his friend anything about the trap. He'd wanted to wait until it had worked. Well, now it had. There could be no doubt that Schafter was a traitor to his country. Dirk would have to decide how to settle the score with him.

The village of De Vlank had an aid committee, set up by a number of enterprising ladies with the aim of offering assistance to the most needy cases that passed through the village. If someone collapsed and couldn't go on, they were admitted to an emergency hospital with six beds, and lovingly nursed back to health for a few days. It was actually Erica who did most of the work. When she'd signed up, the committee had already been in existence for a while, but she had time, was young and strong and knew a thing or two about nursing, so she quickly became one of its mainstays. In return, she had taken bandages for Jack from the committee's limited supplies that winter, which had come in handy.

The committee had also turned the village hall into a "hotel". Straw was laid on the floor and anyone without shelter could sleep there. Erica spent every evening at the village hall, from seven o'clock until just before eight. Together with a small team of first-aiders, she pricked blisters, bandaged sores and put plasters on wounds. Michiel often went to meet her. That had two advantages. Firstly, the dynamo torch could stay at home for longer and, secondly, Erica didn't have to walk back in the dark on her own.

Later, when Michiel thought back to the war, it was often the village hall that came to mind: the first-aiders applying bandages by candlelight, and the murmurs of voices in the darkness. The room had a very special atmosphere. There was so much grief and misery, and yet also a feeling of safety, security for just one night, of friendship and common purpose.

The small stage, where Erica did her work, was illuminated. Otherwise the room was dark, and the rustling of straw was the only sign of people. The minister usually came by at about quarter to eight. He walked down the central aisle towards the light, carefully, so as not to tread on any outstretched hands. With his head bowed, he stood in the light, surrounded by wounds and blisters, and read a few lines from a pocket Bible. And then he spoke a brief word to his invisible congregation.

"Hello, everyone, I can't see you, but I know, I can *feel*, that you're there. We have such great need of one another at times like these..."

Michiel often went a little earlier so that he could listen to the minister. He rarely went to church, but there, in that room, it was different. The minister didn't talk over people's heads; he actually spoke *to* them. And the strange thing was that the people almost seemed to reply with their breathing and their rustling.

Michiel was always surprised that no one ever called out from the darkness: "Hey, you, take your pious sermons and clear off." And no one ever said: "I'm a Catholic, so I don't want to listen to some Protestant preacher." Quite the opposite, in fact. They took hold of his hand or his sleeve and said: "Thank you, Minister, how kind of you to come."

There was once a man who asked him for a page from the Bible, just one page. "I've always been an atheist," he said, "but now I want to carry something of God with me."

Michiel couldn't quite understand it, but he'd always had the feeling that the people in that village hall were *contented*. Why exactly was that? Was it because they were so exhausted from walking and could now stretch out their weary legs on the straw? Was it because *all* of them had it bad? They were hungry. They were far from home. The next day they would have to plod onwards again, diving out of the way as planes approached, wondering yet again if they would find shelter that night. It was strange. His father had been right when he said that war meant hunger, tears, hardship, fear, pain—and yet... In that village hall, Michiel felt that you could also learn from war, that this war had taught him something that would stand him in good stead for the rest of his life.

On the evening of the day the Green Cross building was searched, Michiel was about to go and meet Erica when the doorbell rang. He opened the door, expecting another refugee, but found Schafter standing there in front of him.

"H-Hello there, Schafter, come on in," he stammered.

"No," replied Schafter.

"What can I do for you then?"

"You can listen to me," said Schafter. "You put a note through my door. I don't know what you were thinking, but I don't like it. This afternoon the Green Cross building was raided. Apparently they didn't find anything."

"I put a note in your letter box? Where did you get that idea?"

"I know you did."

"Huh? How?"

"That's none of your business. You probably suspect me of being a traitor. Well, I don't suspect you of the same, so I'm not surprised that there weren't any weapons hidden in that building. But let me assure you that I've never told any secrets to the Germans."

"But... but the raid on the Green Cross building. Why did it happen, then?"

"That's the thing, isn't it?" said Schafter. "You're going to draw conclusions now. The wrong conclusions. I don't know why there was a raid on that building. But I do know one thing: I threw your stupid note in the fire and I didn't tell anyone about it. Not a soul. Got it?"

"No... Um, yes," floundered Michiel.

"Goodbye then."

Schafter angrily turned and disappeared into the night.

Instead of going to meet Erica, Michiel went to his room in the attic to think it over. He sat there on the edge of his bed for a while, staring into the darkness. Yet again, he was baffled. How did Schafter know he'd put the note through his door? No one knew about that, did they? Even Uncle Ben hadn't known he was talking about Schafter. He was certain that he'd seen Schafter at the grocer's. The neighbours? Had a passer-by noticed him? He'd taken a good look around, though, and seen no one. He could have been mistaken, of course, but it was so unlikely. No one spoke to Schafter any more. He couldn't imagine Schafter taking the note around the neighbourhood either, to ask if anyone had seen who'd delivered it. It wasn't that kind of letter.

Was he really that much of an idiot? Everything he did went wrong. Why did it always have to happen to him, Michiel? Hadn't everyone always said his lips were shut tighter than a clam? Hadn't his father and mother said that he could keep a secret even when he was only four years old? Hadn't Erica always accused him of never telling her anything? So why was everything he did so completely transparent to everyone? Well, to Schafter at least. Did the man have second sight? Was he psychic?

His trap had failed—that was obvious. As long as there were so many question marks remaining, he couldn't tell Dirk with any certainty that Schafter was the traitor. In a very grumpy mood, he stomped back downstairs.

"Who was that at the door just now?" his mother asked.

"Santa Claus," Michiel snapped.

"Hey, Michiel..."

"I'm sorry, Mum. It was someone looking for a place to sleep. I sent him to the village hall."

182

Lying came so easily to him these days. It was almost second nature.

"Aren't you going to fetch Erica?" his mother asked. "She doesn't have the torch." Michiel looked at his watch. Two minutes to eight. Just enough time.

Furiously pumping away at the torch as if that might help, he raced out of the door.

14

Ten days went by. The 1st of April came. No one could think of any good jokes. The 2nd of April. The 3rd of April. The rumours about the advancing armies of the Allied Forces became increasingly optimistic. When would Hitler surrender? The war was coming to an end—that much was certain.

For Michiel and Erica, this was a good reason to try to talk Jack out of attempting to return to his squadron. Jack was getting restless. He felt healthy again. Spring was coursing through his veins. It's no easy matter spending an entire winter in a hole under the ground.

"I have to go back and do my bit for the war effort," he said. "They'll never manage without me."

"Why would you take that risk?" Michiel objected. "The war's nearly over—everyone says so."

"Oh, just stay here with us. It'll be fun," said Erica. "We have to celebrate liberation together, don't we? Besides, I want to introduce you to Mother."

But Jack wanted to leave. He was getting increasingly irritable. He was also becoming reckless. One day, Michiel found him waiting for him under a bush outside the spruce plantation. Michiel almost had a heart attack when he heard the words: "Hands up!" and saw a pistol aimed at him from the undergrowth.

Jack just laughed.

Michiel was furious.

"This isn't a joke, Jack," he said. "We're not playing boy scouts on some military training ground in England. Yesterday another twelve people were executed by firing squad in Harderwijk. The war isn't over yet. Quite the opposite, in fact. The Krauts seem to be having more and more fun shooting prisoners and hostages as time goes on."

"Sorry," said Jack guiltily.

That incident made Michiel realize that it really would be better if Jack left. He spoke to Erica about it. At first she didn't want to listen, but when he insisted and said Jack might end up doing something foolish, just because being in the hideout was driving him so crazy, she changed her mind.

"But how?" she asked. "How are we going to get him safely across the rivers? How are we even going to get him safely *to* the rivers in the first place?"

"Uncle Ben," said Michiel.

"Uncle Ben?"

"He's in the resistance. He told me once that he's involved with escape routes for British pilots. And American and Canadian ones, of course. That's what he used to do, at least, when they had to go via Spain or across the North Sea in a boat. I'm pretty sure he'll know of a way to get Jack out."

"Have you already told him about Jack?"

"No, there was no need before. But that's changed now. I'll tell him as soon as he gets here."

Erica sighed. "I suppose we'll have to," she said. "I really wanted Jack to stay until liberation, but fine."

A week later, when Uncle Ben turned up, it was the first thing Michiel asked him. Uncle Ben frowned.

"So, my young friend, you're telling me you've been hiding a British pilot?"

"Yes, that's exactly what I'm telling you."

"For how long?"

"Over six months now."

"And how exactly did you end up with that responsibility?"

"I don't think you need to know that," said Michiel.

Uncle Ben's frown grew deeper.

"Michiel, do you know what you're saying? You want my help to smuggle a pilot out of the country. If they catch me, I'll be up against the wall, no questions asked. That gives me the right to find out first if the man really is a pilot and not, say, a German in disguise, don't you think? It gives me the right to know where he came from, where his plane went down, how he's been looked after so far, who he knows, and so on."

"Well, um, I suppose so..." said Michiel hesitantly.

His old habit of keeping silent, of not saying anything unless it was absolutely necessary, was hard to resist, but he knew Uncle Ben's request was reasonable. Reluctantly, he told Jack and Dirk's story, not revealing that Dirk had killed the German with a billhook. He told him that Dirk had hidden the pilot and looked after him, and he told him about the letter and about Dirk's arrest. Then he explained his own role in the events, and Erica's too.

Uncle Ben placed his hand on Michiel's shoulder.

"You did a man's job," he said. "I'm proud of you."

Michiel blushed. Up until now, he'd focused mainly on the mistakes he'd made. It had never occurred to him that he deserved some praise too.

"So where exactly is this hiding place?" asked Uncle Ben.

"Don't you think it would be better if I tell you at the very last minute, after you've organized his escape? You could get caught. The less you know, the better."

Uncle Ben gave him an approving smile.

"You're remarkably mature for your age, young man," he said. "Most people are blabbermouths. They can't wait to tell everyone all of their business. It's some kind of need to prove themselves, I think. Confident people, strong characters—they don't need that. Their own approval is enough. They don't care about other people's praise or disapproval. I'll get to work right away. But you'll have to help me. What's this pilot of yours wearing?"

"What's left of his uniform and an ancient jacket. Rags, basically."

"He needs to be wearing an ordinary suit that won't stand out. Can you get one to him? Take something from your father's wardrobe."

Michiel nodded.

"There's a camera in my suitcase," Uncle Ben continued. "Do you know how to take photographs? OK, I'll show you. I'm going to need a passport photo for his fake identity card."

Uncle Ben fetched the camera and carefully explained to Michiel how to take the photo. He made him repeat the instructions a few times until he was certain he wouldn't make any mistakes.

"Can you make sure I get the camera back by tomorrow afternoon at the latest?"

"I think so."

"Good. I'm sure I don't need to tell you that your pilot should be wearing civilian clothes when you take the photo, do I?"

"Hm," said Michiel. "It's just as well you mentioned it."

"Photo on Wednesday," mumbled Uncle Ben. "Developed on Thursday, fake ID at the weekend, organize the escape route. Let me see... Then I can probably take him to a safe house on Monday, and they'll take him onwards from there."

"Monday. That soon?" said Michiel, with a little pang in his heart.

"Yes, I think so."

Michiel set straight to work. His father's clothes were far too big for Jack, who had a slim build. But with a jacket that looked a little smaller than the others, and a pair of trousers held on with a belt, it should work. After all, so many people were thinner now, because of the war, that it was perfectly normal for your clothes to swamp your body.

As he was taking the things from the wardrobe, his mother caught him.

She stopped in the doorway. Looked at the clothes spread out on the bed. Opened her mouth and said: "What are you..." Then, thinking better of it, she turned and left the room. Quietly, she closed the door behind her.

Michiel realized that he was a lot like his mother. She could keep silent too. But his mother's silence was about not asking questions—and that seemed even more difficult than not telling secrets.

Taking the photograph went smoothly enough. Jack was excited to hear that he'd be able to leave as soon as Monday. The prospect of danger made his heart beat a little faster. Dirk was actually a bit jealous. He was a lot stronger now and was eager to get back to action too. Unfortunately, though, he still couldn't walk properly. If he reported to the underground, he'd be more of a hindrance than a help.

"This uncle of yours," he asked Michiel, "does he know what he's doing? Has he done this before?"

"It's all he's been doing for years," said Michiel. "If anyone can pull this off, it's him."

Michiel had decided that Erica would take their uncle to the hiding place on Monday. His sister's relationship with

Jack was different from his own. It had been an effort to arrange it that way, but Erica's sad face when she heard about Jack's imminent departure had settled the matter for him.

On Sunday he'd gone to say his own farewells to Jack.

"After liberation, I'll come back to see you all as soon as I can," Jack had said. "And, Michiel, thank you for saving my life."

"Oh, no, I—"

"Yes, you did. Without Dirk and you and Erica, I'd never have survived this war. That's a nice thought, eh? Later, when I'm the prime minister, you'll be able to say, 'If it weren't for us, Britain wouldn't have such a fine leader now.'"

"So long, Jack. Do exactly as my uncle says."

A quick handshake. A nod. Farewell.

Now it was Monday. Uncle Ben and Erica had just left. On foot. They were walking to the woods to fetch Jack. All Erica had to do was show him the way. Then she'd say goodbye and leave in a different direction. Uncle Ben and Jack would walk through the village, surrounded by all the people who were passing through. They'd deliberately chosen the middle of the day, so that they wouldn't stand out. If they were stopped, Jack would show his fake ID and pretend to stutter. Uncle Ben would explain that he had a speech defect. Everything had to go according to plan.

Michiel went to chop wood, behind the shed. From time to time, he looked up at the church clock. The minutes crept by. Uncle Ben and Erica must be there by now. Oh no, not quite. The April sun shone down on the back of his neck. He laid the axe on the ground and sat down on the chopping block, leaning his back against the shed. The exhaustion of a winter full of tension and hard work flooded his body. But now he no longer had the responsibility of looking after Jack. That was a reassuring thought. But he was still going to miss him.

Michiel closed his eyes and turned his face to the sun. The warmth was so pleasant. Did he doze off for a moment? He was startled to hear Jochem's voice, nearby, as if his little brother were bawling in his ear. It took him a moment to realize where the sound was coming from. The shed. The board he was leaning his head against had given way a little, making a gap. At a glance, you couldn't see the crack, as the boards overlapped a little. Jochem was apparently talking to Mother—he could hear every word.

"But I've already looked," whined Jochem. "It's not here."

"You were playing in here though, weren't you?" Mother asked.

"Yes. For a bit."

"And did you go to play with Joost next door?"

"Can't remember. Oh, yes. Yesterday."

"Well, then maybe that's where you left your coat. Let's go and ask."

The voices died away.

Michiel was still a little dozy after his nap, but suddenly he froze. Only his eyes moved, opening wider and wider. That sound... The voices in the shed... The truth dawned on him, so clear, so certain, that not a trace of doubt remained.

He bit the inside of his cheek to break the spell. Then he leapt up and ran to his bike, throwing himself onto the saddle and pedalling like he'd never pedalled before. He had to make it in time. Please, please, if only he could make it in time.

Tyres rattling, he raced along the main road, narrowly missing an old lady who was pushing a doll's pram, swerving past Mr Coenen's dung cart and storming around the corner. No time now for caution, for making sure no one saw him. There was the wood. Would they still be there?

His mind was racing. He knew exactly what he had to do—as clearly as if he'd already seen it in a movie. At full tilt, he took the bend to the left, into the woods. Where he almost collided with Uncle Ben and Jack.

"Michiel, whatever's wrong?" cried Uncle Ben.

Michiel jumped off the bike and grabbed Jack's arm.

"Jack, do you have your pistol?"

"Yes. Why?"

"Quickly. Give it to me."

Looking puzzled, Jack pulled out the gun from under his jacket. Michiel almost tore it from his hands. He flicked off the safety catch, which Jack had taught him how to do, and aimed the gun at Uncle Ben.

"Hands up," he barked.

"What on earth's going on?" said Uncle Ben.

Jack just gasped.

"That man. He's the traitor," panted Michiel. "He's the one who betrayed Dirk and the baroness and Bertus, and he would have taken you straight to the German barracks, Jack."

"You're insane," said Uncle Ben.

"No, I *was* insane," said Michiel, "but I'm not any more."

"Why don't we go back to the hideout?" Jack suggested. "It doesn't seem very safe to me here. Give me the gun. I was our squadron's champion marksman during training."

"As long as you promise to keep it pointed at him at all times."

"I most certainly will."

Jack gave Uncle Ben a push and nodded his head to indicate that he should walk back in the direction they'd just come from. Luckily, there was no sign of anyone else in the woods.

"This is ridiculous," said Uncle Ben. "You can't treat me this way. Michiel's spouting a load of nonsense. I've been in the resistance for four years."

"I'm sure you have," scoffed Michiel. "Four years as a Judas in your own ranks. How many victims do you have on your conscience?"

"Don't listen to him," said Uncle Ben to Jack, who waved the gun to make him move faster.

"If there's one person I trust in this world, it's Michiel," said Jack. "Go on, keep walking."

Uncle Ben doubled his protests when he had to crawl through the trees on his stomach, but it didn't do him any good. When they reached the hideout, Dirk was amazed to see them.

"It seems we have your traitor here," said Jack. "Here you go, all in one piece, all yours."

He handed Dirk the pistol.

"I've never seen that man before," said Uncle Ben.

"That's... true," said Dirk hesitantly.

"Even so, he's still the one who betrayed you to the Nazis," growled Michiel.

"Rubbish," said Uncle Ben.

"Why don't we search his pockets?" suggested Michiel.

"Good idea."

Uncle Ben protested vehemently, but the other three men ignored him. And then the evidence appeared. A card entitling the holder to ride in German military vehicles. A list of telephone numbers for the German authorities. A letter from a German girlfriend in Hannover. And the icing on the cake: a letter from the SS, inviting the esteemed Mr Van Hierden to deliver the British pilot to the barracks at De Vlank.

"Is that his name? Van Hierden?" asked Jack.

"Yes. Ben van Hierden. My so-called uncle. He's been a close friend of my parents for many, many years. I'll never call him 'uncle' again, as long as I live."

"But I wonder," Dirk whispered threateningly, "just how much longer his life will be?"

Ben van Hierden wiped the sweat from his forehead with the back of his hand.

"You... You can't prove anything," he stammered.

"Really?" said Dirk. "Isn't this enough proof? Tell us, Michiel, how did you find out?"

Michiel found it hard to explain everything clearly. The wild bike ride, the fear, but above all his fury about his so-called uncle's betrayal and his own frustration at the way he'd been fooled—it was all making his head spin.

"The sticks of last resort..." he began.

He tried to get his thoughts straight.

"I thought my Dutch was getting pretty good," said Jack, "but 'sticks of last resort'? That's a new one on me."

"This morning I was out behind the shed, chopping logs for the fire," Michiel told him. "That's where the chopping block is, and where we stack the logs. We always do the chopping out back. Suddenly I heard voices, very clearly, but I couldn't see anyone around. Turned out it was Mother and Jochem, who were in the shed, looking for Jochem's coat or something. I could hear them perfectly, because there's a gap in the boards. Then I remembered the morning when Dirk gave me the letter. It was in the shed. That same morning, a little earlier, that man over there"—he pointed at Van Hierden—"had burnt all the thin pieces of wood that Mother keeps in the chest by the stove for emergencies. We call them the sticks of last resort. I'd told him he'd have to chop some more. I can still see him walking out there with the axe. He must have sat down on the chopping block for a rest, like I did this morning. And that was how he heard what Dirk said to me.

"Now let's just go through exactly what Dirk told me. Firstly, he said there was going to be a raid on the rations office in Lagezande, and three men would be involved. Dirk and his friend walked into a trap and the Krauts knew there was supposed to be a third man. Secondly, Dirk mentioned Bertus van Gelder. I was supposed to give Bertus the letter if anything went wrong. Van Hierden heard his name. But he also wanted to get his hands on the letter. He didn't know that I'd hidden the letter in the shed. Or to be more precise—in the chicken coop."

Ben van Hierden couldn't help clicking his fingers.

"No, you didn't think of that, did you?" sneered Michiel. Then he continued, "That night he searched my room. I caught him at it. He reacted very quickly, said he wanted to look up a word in my English dictionary. The English word for *dynamiet*. He might have been better off looking up how to say *verrader* in English."

"Traitor," Jack said helpfully.

"My goodness, Jack," joked Dirk. "You speak such good English."

"Shall I continue?" asked Michiel.

"I do wish you wouldn't play with the pistol like that," said Ben van Hierden. "Guns do sometimes go off, you know."

"That wouldn't be such a bad solution," Dirk said darkly. "But I would rather like to have free hands. Let's tie him up."

Five minutes later, Van Hierden's hands were tied behind his back and a rope was knotted around his ankles and knees. Then Michiel went on with his story.

"When he couldn't find the letter, I imagine his reasoning went like this: let's wait until the end of tomorrow to raid Bertus van Gelder's place. Then we'll find the letter with him. He assumed I'd deliver it straightaway. And I'm sure you want to know why I didn't, don't you?"

Ben van Hierden didn't reply.

"I had all kinds of bad luck that day," Michiel continued. "You know that Schafter cycled with me to Councillor Van Kleiweg's, and then he saw me again later that day. But that didn't mean he knew about Bertus. So it was pure coincidence, Dirk. You were right about that."

"But he showed the Germans the way to Driekusmanswegje, didn't he?" objected Dirk.

"Maybe they asked for directions. It's no secret. No reason why he shouldn't tell them. Anyway, he could still easily be a friend of the Germans. Everyone says he is. But there's no way he could have betrayed Bertus. That man over there—he was the only one who knew. And then there was the question of the Koppel ferry. On the evening of the day when I took the Rotterdammers over the river, Van Hierden happened to come by. He hadn't heard about my father's death yet. And he seemed so upset that, to cheer him up, I told him about—"

"But I *was* upset," said Ben van Hierden. "I always liked your father."

"Then perhaps you should have let the Krauts know that. I'm sure it would have helped."

"That's the thing, though," muttered Ben van Hierden. "That's why I was so shaken up. I'd neglected to tell the commander to keep his hands off the mayor."

"And what about the town clerk and the minister and the others? They didn't matter, eh?" said Michiel furiously. "It was alright for them to die. The town clerk's wife is in a psychiatric clinic now. Did you know that? She's never going to get over it."

Ben van Hierden didn't reply.

"Anyway, to cheer him up, I threw caution to the wind and told him about how the baroness was putting one over on the Krauts. You all know what happened then. The next morning, the soldiers turned up and closed it all down. And I was such an idiot for suspecting Schafter."

For a while, they were all sunk in their own thoughts. Jack was thinking that this meant the end of his escape to the south. Ben van Hierden was frantically searching for a way out of the tricky situation. Dirk was trying to decide what they should do with the traitor. And Michiel was wondering how this man, a man he'd called Uncle his entire life, a man he'd always liked so much, had come to stoop so very low.

"I made sure you were kept out of everything," said Ben van Hierden.

"That should have been a clue," said Michiel. "A few times I was sure they'd come for me. So why didn't you give them my name?"

"Because I've always been so fond of you."

"Careful, Michiel," said Dirk. "Don't let him get to you."

"Why did you do it?" asked Michiel. "Were the Germans paying you?"

"No," replied Ben van Hierden, with a fanatical gleam in his eyes. "I did it because Hitler's such a great man. He understands that some races were created to rule and others to serve. There's a good reason why the Slavic people got that name—they're only fit to be slaves. And the French and the Italians and the Spanish are weaklings too. The Jews are so inferior that they deserve to be wiped out entirely."

Michiel remembered Jitzchak Kleerkoper's fine, intelligent face.

"The English might be worth something if they weren't so decadent," Van Hierden continued.

"Thanks very much," said Jack with a grimace.

"But the greatest nation, the master race—that's the Germans. They're tall and blond, they have the best engineers and scientists, they've produced the greatest composers. And they're military men. No other army is as disciplined, as—"

"Just shut up!" said Dirk suddenly. "I can't listen to this claptrap any longer."

He rubbed the scar that ran from his left ear to his nose.

"What are we going to do with him?" asked Jack.

"That's what I've been wondering too," replied Dirk.

"There really is only one option," said Jack casually.

Dirk nodded.

"Michiel, you can't allow them to do this," growled Ben van Hierden.

"To do what?"

"To..."

"Do the two of you want to shoot him?" Michiel asked quietly.

Dirk shrugged.

"Do you have a better idea?"

Again, silence fell in the hideout.

"You can do it," Jack said to Dirk after a while. "You're the one who's suffered most because of him."

"Me? No, please, go ahead. You're the soldier."

"No," said Jack, "that wasn't part of the training."

"Can't we hand him over to the resistance?" suggested Michiel. "Mr Postma can decide what needs to be done."

Dirk had to think about that.

"But how are we going to get him to the resistance? And how can we convince them that he's a collaborator? Aren't we running an unnecessary risk by involving others?"

They couldn't make up their minds. Jack thought they should ask Erica's opinion too. Finally they decided to sleep on it. Van Hierden could stay tied up in the hideout, although the space was cramped for three people.

"Oh well," said Jack, "there's not much room in a cockpit either. And where would I be now if Michiel couldn't ride his bike quite so fast?"

"See you tomorrow," said Michiel. "I'll tell Erica what's going on."

He crawled through the trees, climbed onto his bike and cycled home. Even with all the bitterness he felt, he was relieved, because the uncertainty and the mysteries were over. He understood now how Ben van Hierden had been able to organize a letter from Jack's mother so quickly. He'd obviously told the Germans not to get in the way of the Red Cross, so that Michiel would be impressed by his connections. And it was indeed that quick exchange of letters with Jack's mother that had made him trust Uncle Ben all the more.

There was only one question still buzzing around inside his head. It was about the Green Cross building. *How had Schafter known that Michiel had written that letter?* He shook his head. No matter how hard he tried, he couldn't work it out.

15

The next day, they all met up at the hiding place, including Erica, who had been deeply shocked to hear that Uncle Ben was a collaborator. She could still hardly believe it. Now that they were in the hideout together, she avoided looking at him.

Dirk had thought long and hard. He shared his conclusions with the others.

"Yes, I think we should give him to Mr Postma," he said. "He could have information that might be important for the resistance. Mr Postma will just have to get it out of him. Hopefully the war will be over soon, and then they can hand him over to the authorities. The judge can decide what his punishment should be. But I'll be only too happy to testify against him."

Michiel thought that Dirk had maybe chosen that course of action because he couldn't carry out the sentence himself. The same probably went for Jack. Dirk clearly hadn't even considered asking Erica or Michiel.

"OK?" said Dirk.

He looked around. Everyone nodded.

"How are we going to get him out of here?" asked Michiel.

"I suggest you take a letter from me to Mr Postma," said Dirk. "With any luck, Postma will know of a place where he can hide Van Hierden. You'll have to ask him if he's willing to come to the edge of Dagdaler Wood to fetch the prisoner. And, with the help of the pistol, I'll take him from here to the meeting point."

"That'll never work," said Jack. "Your hands are still shaking far too much to hold onto the pistol. I'll do it."

But Dirk shook his head.

"It's not a good idea for Postma to meet you. One of us will have to do it. I'd rather he didn't know exactly where our hiding place is either. I trust him, but the fewer people who know, the better."

"I'll do it," said Michiel.

"You sure you're up to it?"

"Of course I am. Why wouldn't I be?"

"Good, then that's agreed."

"But if the Germans stop me and find the letter, we've had it," said Michiel. "So wouldn't it be better for me to pass on a message to Mr Postma rather than taking a letter?"

"He might not believe you. I'll try to write the letter in such a way that it won't mean anything to anyone except him."

They all agreed on the plan. All Dirk wrote in his note was:

M. v. B. is completely trustworthy, signed White Leghorn.

Which, as Mr Postma would know, actually meant "signed Dirk Knopper".

Michiel found Mr Postma at home. He read the note, and then gave Michiel a searching look.

"Do you know who White Leghorn is?"

Michiel nodded.

"Is he in prison?"

"He escaped."

"Thank God," said Mr Postma. "Where is he now?"

Michiel looked his old teacher straight in the eyes, without saying a word.

"Fine. So what can I do for you, Michiel?"

The young resistance fighter told him about the collaborator and what he'd done. "And now we'd like to hand him over to you," he said, finishing his story.

After some thought, Mr Postma agreed to take the prisoner. He'd come and fetch him at half-past seven the following evening, at the agreed meeting point.

"How? On foot?" asked Michiel.

"Yes."

"Aren't you worried he'll escape in the village, with all those people passing through?"

"It's already getting dark by then. There won't be many people about. Besides, I don't need to use the main road. The busiest part of the route will be the old station road. It should be pretty quiet, but there's still a risk. Would you come along? Then we can make him walk between us."

"Good idea."

"Fine. I'll see you tomorrow evening, then."

Ben van Hierden had scented his chance to escape. In the short stretch from the hideout to the edge of the woods, he'd be alone with Michiel. He'd surely find some way to do it then.

Jack crawled with them to the path, where he handed Michiel the pistol.

"If he tries to make a run for it, don't hesitate to shoot," he said.

Michiel nodded, as calmly as he could. Would he really be able to do it? To shoot the man he'd loved like an uncle for so long?

Holding the pistol under his jacket, Michiel made Van Hierden walk a few steps ahead. They were barely out of Jack's sight when the man turned around.

"Michiel, do we really have to walk through the woods like this?" he asked with a sigh. "Have you forgotten all the pleasant walks we've had together?"

"Keep going," growled Michiel.

But Ben van Hierden did not keep going. He sat down on a fallen tree. Michiel took out the pistol and aimed it at the man's head.

"I'll shoot," he said, but he didn't sound too sure.

"I don't believe you," said Van Hierden. "You can't shoot me. We've been friends for too long. Come and sit beside me for a moment and let's talk."

"I told you to get up and keep walking," said Michiel, with a tremble in his voice.

"Listen, Michiel, please try to understand me. I believe that the German system of national socialism is the best thing for our country and for the world. That is possible, isn't it? You don't have to agree with me, but someone can honestly have that opinion, can't they? Right? Well, that's how I feel. And doesn't that make it my duty to do whatever I can to help the Germans spread their system all over the world? Isn't it a question of honour and conscience?"

"No," said Michiel, "no one's honour and conscience should force them to betray their land and their fellow countrymen. Or to get Willem Stomp shot and Dirk Knopper's toes smashed."

A feeling of triumph shot through Van Hierden. He had got the boy to talk—and to see him as a human being once again. Now there was no way Michiel would be able to bring himself to shoot him.

"Terrible things happen in every war," he continued. "I don't like it either, but they still happen all the same. Do you really think the Russians and the Americans are such angels?"

"They're fighting for a just cause," said Michiel. "But I'm not interested in talking to you. Get up and start walking."

"What do you think those people from the resistance will do to me? Exactly the same as what happened to

Dirk. They'll torture me until they think I've told them everything that's worth knowing. Then they'll shoot me."

"It's what you deserve," said Michiel, but he was starting to hesitate. Was Mr Postma really capable of that? He couldn't imagine it. On the other hand, could he ever have imagined that Uncle Ben was a collaborator?

"I'm going to walk off down that path over there," said Ben van Hierden calmly, "and you're not going to shoot. You're going to say I escaped because a German patrol came through the woods or something like that. I promise you'll never see me again."

He had stood up and was walking slowly backwards down the path, his eyes fixed on Michiel's. Michiel stood there with the pistol in his hand and didn't move. Could he shoot at that familiar face? He thought about his father, about the baroness, about Dirk, about Bertus and Jannechien. What good would it do them if Ben van Hierden were killed? But Jack... Jack would be caught, of course. Van Hierden knew about the hideout. And Erica and Michiel—they'd be arrested and shot too. Still he didn't move.

And his mother... his mother would receive another letter, maybe even two letters in the same envelope, politely informing her that her daughter and her son... She would grit her teeth and send Jochem to join the underground. The madness of that thought, a boy of six as a resistance fighter, was what it took to break the spell. As Michiel pictured his mother's look of determination, the smile on Van Hierden's face seemed to turn into a sly grin.

Michiel stepped forward and pulled the trigger. The bullet didn't hit, but the shot sounded incredibly loud in the quiet of the evening. Van Hierden's hands shot up.

"Now walk," hissed Michiel, "or I'll shoot you dead, for sure."

The traitor realized that his plan had failed. Obediently, he headed in the direction Michiel pointed. They soon met Mr Postma, who, alerted by the shot, had run towards them.

"He tried to escape," Michiel explained.

Mr Postma was wearing a raincoat with large pockets, his hand clutching a pistol inside the right one. He walked close beside Van Hierden, pressing the barrel of the gun through the fabric of his coat into the man's hip.

"I'll shoot first and then warn you," he said.

Michiel walked on the other side of his former uncle. None of them spoke a word. Twice they saw someone they knew, and they nodded and smiled as naturally as they could. After a while, they reached the road to the station. But something was different. What was it?

"Munitions trucks," whispered Mr Postma.

There were five camouflaged trucks standing beneath the trees, about a hundred yards apart.

"Are they dangerous?" asked Michiel.

"Very. One lit cigarette could cause a disaster."

A little later, Michiel heard a quiet droning in the distance.

"I think Rinus de Raat is about to pay us a visit," he said.

Mr Postma stopped.

"You're right. A Spitfire. That's a problem."

Michiel thought his reaction was a little extreme. He'd seen British planes in action so many times before. The noise swiftly came closer.

"Quick! Take cover!" said Mr Postma. When Michiel didn't move, he yelled: "Don't you get it? If that plane fires even a single round into one of those trucks, half of the village will go up in flames."

He pushed Ben van Hierden into one of the holes at the side of the road.

"Keep down," he growled. "I've got my gun on you."

Then he jumped into the next hole, and Michiel took the one after that.

Mr Postma peered out over the edge of the hole, closely watching Van Hierden.

Soon the plane came thundering over their heads. They all ducked, but there was no sound of shots. The plane disappeared. Michiel began to climb out, but Mr Postma signalled at him to stay down.

"He could come back," he shouted.

He was right. The pilot must have seen something suspicious. He made a sharp turn above the village and came flying back along the road, lower than before. As the terrifying noise swelled, Michiel and Mr Postma ducked into their holes. But Ben van Hierden seized his chance. He leapt up and, before they even noticed, he'd already zigzagged his way about twenty yards down the road. Mr Postma wanted to shoot, but he was scared of hitting one of the trucks. He might as well have done it though, as the Spitfire unleashed a hail of bullets towards the vehicles. A deafening noise. It was as if the ground split apart. Michiel and Mr Postma lay curled up like hedgehogs in the bottom of their holes—it's incredible how small you can make yourself when you need to. Two trucks were blown to smithereens—fortunately the two that were furthest away from Michiel and Mr Postma. Huge craters in the ground marked the spots where they had been. A tree lay halfway across the road. Three houses were now piles of rubble. The devastation was shocking.

When the sound of the explosions had died away, Michiel and Mr Postma emerged from their hiding places, their faces pale. Ben van Hierden had been wiped off the face of the earth, so thoroughly that it would be hard to find any part of him to bury. People came running from every direction, diving onto the smoking heaps of rubble, searching for survivors. Michiel wanted to join them, but Mr Postma said, "We need to get away. There's enough help here."

"Why? Van Hierden's dead, isn't he?"

"Our guns. If they stop us and search us, we've had it."

"Of course. Yes, yes, you're right."

They each went their own way. Mr Postma headed home, and Michiel went back to the hideout to return the pistol to Jack and Dirk and to tell them what had happened. In spite of the shock, he felt relieved. Ben van Hierden would not be able to do any more harm. But he was tired. Tired from all the danger and the tension, from the fear and the responsibility. When, when, when would this terrible war finally be over?

16

The Van Beusekoms were just eating lunch when a vanguard of five British tanks entered the village. Mother was the first to notice the unusual vehicles. They looked less bulky than the German tanks, more nimble, more elegant. In every gun turret stood a man in a light-coloured jacket with a beret perched at a jaunty angle over one ear. She jumped to her feet and, shouting louder than her children had ever heard, cried out: "Our liberators!"

People wrapped in orange sashes and Dutch flags poured out of the houses and onto the streets. They climbed onto the tanks and hugged the soldiers. The hiding places opened up—and out came the Jewish people and the escaped prisoners and the hidden pilots. There was singing and dancing and celebration.

It was soon discovered that not a single German was left in the entire village, and the barracks had been abandoned. The night before, everyone and everything that was German had disappeared across the IJssel.

The men from the underground finally surfaced. They wore special orange bands on their arms to show that they'd been members of the resistance. The men who had been fighting in secret for a long time, who had lived in danger for years, were tired and humble. Now they simply did what had to be done, and they left it at that. Those who had joined the resistance only in recent weeks, however, when the war was clearly coming to an end, were full of stories and paraded around the streets at every opportunity. They also had fun bringing in everyone who was suspected of having been too friendly with the Germans. The girls who had gone out with German soldiers had their heads shaved. Men were hoisted onto the handlebars of motorbikes and driven through the village with their hands up, before being imprisoned in the school. Some of them deserved no better, while others had just been friendly to the Germans because they were scared, but had done nothing else wrong.

Schafter was one of those taken for a ride on the front of a motorbike. However, that turned out to be a serious mistake. He'd actually had three Jewish people hiding in his house all along. He was soon released, with an apology. Michiel went to visit him at home to say how sorry he was for having suspected him.

"You thought I was the one who told them about the Koppel ferry, eh?" said Schafter. "After all, we'd spoken about it only that morning."

"I'm so sorry," said Michiel shamefacedly. "It's just that you asked so many questions. And everyone said you were hand in glove with the Germans and... well, to be honest, that's what it looked like."

Schafter nodded. "The thing was, I had those people in my house. They'd been with me since 1942. At a certain point I realized that the Germans were getting suspicious. So, to be on the safe side, I pretended to be a friend of theirs. I did little favours for them, trivial things, of course. Obviously I never gave them any information about anyone."

"Did you tell them to go to Bertus van Gelder's house?"

"Huh? No."

"Jannechien heard that, on the day her husband was taken in, you were seen chatting with the Germans."

"Oh, that's what you're talking about. They knew me, so they asked me the way. What I mean is that they asked me if I knew where Driekusmanswegje was. And, of course, I told them where it was. They could have found it just as easily on a map."

"But how on earth did you know I was the one who posted that letter through your door?" asked Michiel.

"Because of the people who were in hiding in my house. We'd made a peephole by the front door, just for emergencies. They heard footsteps on the gravel and looked to see who was coming. I could tell from their description that it must be you. And I knew you were suspicious of me because of the ferry business."

"I see," said Michiel. "I really am sorry that I suspected you. But you were just so... curious about everything."

"It's in my nature," said Schafter with a grin.

"Aren't you angry about the way they treated you?"

"Not really," said Schafter. "I was scared I'd fall off the motorbike, that's all. I knew it would all turn out fine in the end. Do you know who it was who came to get me?"

"Yes. I saw you going past. It was Dries Grotendorst, wasn't it?"

"That's right. The Grotendorsts kept a motorbike hidden under their hay shed for the last few years. They made a pile of money on the black market too. I heard they were asking for twelve new pre-war bed sheets in exchange for a pound of butter."

"Really? But there wasn't much profiteering around here," said Michiel.

"No, the local farmers were honest and decent for the main part," Schafter agreed. "But not the Grotendorsts. Dries was a member of the resistance for precisely twenty-two days. Not long enough for him to know I'd been a member for three and a half years. Oh well... At least he's pretty safe on a motorbike."

"Would you believe I always suspected Dries was a big shot in the resistance? It just goes to show how wrong you can be. Thank God it's all over now," said Michiel.

Schafter nodded. "You can say that again," he replied. "But still... how many people can really be happy? The people who hid in my house are free to walk the streets for the first time in three years. Are they happy? In a way, I suppose, yes, but then... They're probably the only members of their family who are still alive. That's a very sad place to start over again."

Michiel thought about his father.

"And you know exactly what I'm talking about, of course," said Schafter.

"Yes, it's hard, especially for Mother. Do you remember those two farmers' wives I took over on the ferry? They were actually a Mr Kleerkoper and his son. Someone brought a message from Den Hulst this morning to say that they survived the war. But yes, they..."

He didn't finish his sentence.

Schafter nodded. "It's terrible what the Nazis have done to the Jews," he said. "So many deaths."

Michiel headed home. In spite of Schafter's sombre words, in spite of his mother's sad eyes, a feeling of happiness was bubbling up inside him. It was over, finally over. Hitler had been defeated. An end had come to the shooting and the murders and the torture. Dirk was with his parents, safe and sound. Jack was back with his squadron and wrote Erica long, loving letters full of mistakes. Van Dijk the ferryman had died in a concentration camp in Germany, but Bertus was back with his Jannechien. The days of starvation were over. There were delicious things to eat, like "corned beef", whatever that might actually be. The Allied soldiers lived in luxury. They wore casual, sporty gear—such a breath of fresh air after the Germans' loath-some, stiff uniforms! They joked with the girls, dished out cigarettes and cans of food and raced around in small open vehicles, which they called Jeeps.

Life had colour again. There were many stories of death, but also stories about people who had miraculously survived the war. Newspapers were being published again and you were allowed to read them right in the middle of the street if you wanted. What a difference from the illegal newssheets—being caught in possession of one of those could have got you killed. And then there were all the parties. People couldn't get enough of dancing and singing, of fun and laughter. They had five years to catch up on. Peacetime was met with joy, peace after a war the like of which should never, ever be seen again.

A few months later. The war with Japan was now over too. America had succeeded in creating two terrible, devastating bombs. Atom bombs. It was deemed necessary to drop them on the Japanese cities of Hiroshima and Nagasaki. Those two cities, with all their men, women and children, were wiped out, and Japan surrendered. The damaged world could now start licking its wounds.

One evening, Michiel and Dirk went for a walk around the village. It was a slow process. Dirk's right foot was in plaster. At the hospital they'd broken his toes all over again and then straightened them, this time under anaesthesia. If his right foot healed properly, they'd do the left one next. They were optimistic that he'd be able to walk normally again in about a year. For now, though, it was just one step at a time, with the help of a walking stick.

In the distance, they saw Gert Verkoren approaching, an athletic young man of around twenty-five.

"You see Gert Verkoren over there?" asked Dirk.

"Yes. What about him?"

"He was the third man in the raid on the rations office in Lagezande."

"The man you didn't give away?"

Dirk nodded.

Gert had come closer now.

"Evening, Gert."

"Hello, Dirk. Michiel."

He stopped for a chat.

"So how's your foot, Dirk?"

"Not so bad. Next year I'll be running the race around the village again."

"If it weren't for me, you'd be running it this year," said Gert, "and winning it too. You've no idea how grateful I am, Dirk."

"There's really no need," said Dirk. "I was unlucky and you weren't. That's all there is to it."

Humbly, he changed the subject.

"Hey, Gert, that's a nice shirt you're wearing."

"Yeah, thanks. My girlfriend made it for me out of parachute silk. Would you believe I came across a dead Kraut wrapped up in a British parachute? The Kraut wasn't much good to me, but the parachute came in handy."

Michiel gaped, but no sound came out. Dirk laid his hand on his arm as if to say, "Let me do the talking."

Calmly he asked, "When was that?"

"Just before the raid. I got out of the area pretty quickly after that. Didn't come back to De Vlank until after liberation. The parachute was still waiting for me in the barn, under the chicken feed."

"Did you know..." Dirk began, but then he stopped.

"Know what?"

"Oh, it doesn't matter. Come on, Michiel, let's get going. Evening, Gert."

"See you around."

As they strolled on, Dirk gave Michiel an apologetic smile. "There's no sense talking about it now, eh?" he said.

"No," replied Michiel. "There's only one thing now that makes any sense."

"What's that?"

"Never fighting *in* another war ever again, only fighting *against* war."

"You're absolutely right," said Dirk.

17

Many years have passed since then. Michiel is now an old man of eighty-nine. He reads the newspapers and he knows that since his walk with Dirk that evening, there has been fighting in Hungary, Vietnam, Korea, China, Northern Ireland, the former Yugoslavia, Turkey, Cambodia, Indonesia, Nepal, Bangladesh, India, Pakistan, Sri Lanka, Myanmar, Bhutan, Papua New Guinea, Taiwan, Jordan, Lebanon, Libya, the Congo, Angola, Burundi, Côte d'Ivoire, Liberia, Sudan, Ethiopia, Nigeria, Senegal, Somalia, Rwanda, Uganda, Eritrea, Yemen, Niger, Djibouti, Tanzania, Kenya, Mali, Ecuador, the Dominican Republic, Cuba, Honduras, Haiti, Columbia, Venezuela, Guatemala, Peru, Bolivia, Mexico, the Falkland Islands, East Timor, Afghanistan, Iran, Iraq, Russia, Chechnya, Georgia, Israel, Algeria, Egypt, Ukraine, Syria and many, many other countries.

PUSHKIN CHILDREN'S BOOKS

We created Pushkin Children's Books to share tales from different languages and cultures with younger readers, and to open the door to the wide, colourful worlds these stories offer.

From picture books and adventure stories to fairy tales and classics, and from fifty-year-old bestsellers to current huge successes abroad, the books on the Pushkin Children's list reflect the very best stories from around the world, for our most discerning readers of all: children.

THE BEGINNING WOODS
MALCOLM MCNEILL

'I loved every word and was envious of quite a few... A
modern classic. Rich, funny and terrifying'
Eoin Colfer

THE RED ABBEY CHRONICLES
MARIA TURTSCHANINOFF

1 · *Maresi*

2 · *Naondel*

'Embued with myth, wonder, and told with
a dazzling, compelling ferocity'
Kiran Millwood Hargrave, author of *The Girl of Ink and Stars*

THE LETTER FOR THE KING
TONKE DRAGT

'*The Letter for the King* will get pulses racing... Pushkin
Press deserves every praise for publishing this beautifully
translated, well-presented and captivating book'
The Times

THE SECRETS OF THE WILD WOOD
TONKE DRAGT

'Offers intrigue, action and escapism'
Sunday Times

THE SONG OF SEVEN
TONKE DRAGT

'A cracking adventure... so nail-biting you'll need to wear protective gloves'
The Times

THE MURDERER'S APE
JAKOB WEGELIUS

'A thrilling adventure. Prepare to meet the remarkable
Sally Jones; you won't soon forget her'
Publishers Weekly